Not the Apocalypse I Was Hoping For

UNIVERSITY OF CALGARY
Press

NOT THE
APOCALYPSE
I WAS
HOPING FOR

LESLIE
GREENTREE

Brave & Brilliant Series
ISSN 2371-7238 (Print) ISSN 2371-7246 (Online)

University of Calgary Press
2500 University Drive NW
Calgary, Alberta
Canada T2N 1N4
press.ucalgary.ca

LIBRARY AND ARCHIVES CANADA CATALOGUING IN PUBLICATION

Title: Not the apocalypse I was hoping for / Leslie Greentree.
Names: Greentree, Leslie, author.
Series: Brave & brilliant series ; no. 27.
Description: Series statement: Brave & brilliant series ; no. 27
Identifiers: Canadiana (print) 20220165556 | Canadiana (ebook) 20220165564 | ISBN
    9781773853697 (softcover) | ISBN 9781773853703 (PDF) | ISBN 9781773853710 (EPUB)
Subjects: LCGFT: Short stories.
Classification: LCC PS8563.R43 N68 2022 | DDC C813/.6—dc23

The University of Calgary Press acknowledges the support of the Government of Alberta
through the Alberta Media Fund for our publications. We acknowledge the financial support
of the Government of Canada. We acknowledge the financial support of the Canada Council
for the Arts for our publishing program.

Printed and bound in Canada by Marquis
This book is printed on 55lb Enviro Book Natural paper

Editing by Aritha van Herk
Copyediting by Naomi K. Lewis
Cover photo of cloche and flowers by Kristina Skoreva on Unsplash
Cover photo of bird by Joshua J. Cotten on Upsplash
Cover design, page design, and typesetting by Melina Cusano

For Gerry, Mickey, Blaine.

Contents

Exit interview #1

Only my mother could turn her impending death into performance art and get a fucking grant for it. I don't know what I expected once we got through the initial shock that she was dying — maybe that we'd finally spend some time together, have those mother-daughter conversations you witness in all the death movies. But that's not the way my mother operates.

By week three, she was madly taking notes — she was breathless with excitement. Maybe part of the breathlessness was due to the lung cancer, but her behaviour was otherwise no different from the usual obsessive-frenetic activity that accompanied the birth of every new project. Except, of course, she had to take breaks between scribbling notes to ingest drugs and go to dozens of doctor's appointments, and she'd been instructed to nap more. Except, of course, this time the project was her death.

"Exit Interview," she called it.

I should have expected to come home from work and find Anthony in our house. But I didn't — she hadn't told me she was granting interviews. My chest tightened at the sight of him perched at the edge of the soft grey couch. My mother sat upright on her red chaise lounge, legs neatly crossed, her watercolour scarf slipping off one pale shoulder. Etta James played softly in the background.

"What are you doing here?"

Anthony pushed himself off the couch and pressed my fingers with his small, soft hands. "Your mother has been telling me about her new project," he said. "It sounds —" Here he paused, his enthusiasm for the project at war with the death timer that necessitated it.

"Yes, it does sound, doesn't it?" I said. I pulled my hand away. "I'm sorry I was off stage for the big reveal."

Anthony wrote about my mother long before she was famous. He called her a bright new light in the theatrical scene. After a show last year, I saw them backstage; my mother glowed the way actors do when they come off stage, still suffused with the energy of her performance. She had her hand on his arm — nothing inappropriate, but I saw the look in his eyes. She said, "You've always been so good to me, Anthony," and he glowed back at her as he nodded. Her face shifted; a micro-expression no one but I would have caught. From that point on, Anthony was the first media person she called with her news, but I never saw her touch him again.

My mother let Anthony out and came into the kitchen as I was dumping macaroni into a stainless-steel pot. Boiling water splashed onto my thumb, and I hissed. "What sort of sauce do you want?"

"You're angry."

"For fuck's sake, Mom. You're dying, you've started some death art project, and you want to — what — bring in a photographer to take pictures of me crying and holding your hand? No way."

"I know you don't like the spotlight, Camille. You won't be in the article, but people need to know."

"Know what?"

The doorbell rang. Katherine, another arts reporter who loved my mother. The music shifted to Dinah Washington.

"Olivia is leaving you the most marvelous gift with this installation," Katherine said. "The ability to speak with her any time you need to." The floral scarf around her neck was meant to look casually tossed, but it bunched at her neck; my mother's fingers twitched.

"I can't talk," I said. "The pasta's getting mushy."

My mother gazed at me compassionately. It would have been more effective if I hadn't seen her use that particular move on stage so often. Derek and I used to call that look her Jesus eyes, full of love, but with a determined, global mission that trumped petty obstacles like individual feelings.

The timer beeped in the kitchen, and I pushed past them. My mother sighed and smoothed her own gauzy green and blue scarf back on her shoulder.

In the first weeks after we discovered that my seemingly healthy mother had less than a year to live, she brooded. I brooded, too. I was frightened, and shellshocked. I tried to imagine what must be going through her mind. When I thought of her death, my mind veered from bedside death scenes and skipped to colourful funeral tableaux filled with dramatic speeches. My mother was always giving one of them.

The house was quiet those first weeks. I made her soups, memorized the various drugs she'd been given and what she was to take at which times. I never saw her take them.

I told my boss. That was a horrifying scene — me snotting all over my sleeve, him pushing a box of tissues at me, promising anything to get me to stop crying and the hell out of his office. I sat in the parking lot dabbing makeup around my puffy eyes, then drove home to tell my mother I would have all the time off I needed to drive her to doctor appointments.

"That's sweet," she said. "But I've already got a dozen people who've promised to drive me whenever and wherever. Theatre people have such flexible schedules."

She pulled a piece of paper from a neat stack on the table. "Remember Janet? She was my stage manager for that piece with the performance poets. Remember how she found that old washing machine and got it jerry-rigged like a fountain?" She smiled at the list in her hand. "Caleb and Jonathan. Patricia. And Patrick, Kate, Nelson . . . God, look at all these names. I'd have to get cancer three times to use them all."

3

The buy-in for her Exit Interview installation was equally enthusiastic — Tom, a lighting and set designer she worked with regularly, dropped every nonurgent project to get busy with plans. She huddled with her dialect coach, Therese, for hours while I was at work.

I don't know if my mother slept much. When I got up each morning, she'd be at the kitchen table, coffee in hand, poring over diagrams and notes, Paloma Faith or Hercules and Love Affair playing in the background. When I came home, she'd be on the phone, or working in her office-slash-studio. Whether she was closed in her studio with someone or alone, I would hear her voice from behind the door. And that only sounds weird if you've never lived with a performer — my mother had been diligently, obsessively listening to her own voice her entire life — all in the name of art, of course.

Artists came and went at all hours, and I went to work every day, and when I was at home, my mother and I talked about soup and accents, and my brother was still reliably absent; there were moments when all this flurry simply seemed like the most current in a long line of projects. Those were the moments when I noticed that her costumes were evolving, that her unkempt hair looked artfully abandoned. Was it wrong of me to roll my eyes?

You don't know my mother, so don't judge me. You may think you know my mother. You've likely seen her perform. She's famous; long before her illness, critics applauded her bravery, her astonishing truth telling. Or maybe you think you'll get to know her better soon, since after her death you'll be able to go to the museum's art gallery and hear her voice any time you want, offering you apologies, or absolution, or love, in her throaty stage voice. You can ask questions, moan and wail, stare at all the images of her while she talks to you from The Great Beyond. Whatever your particular grief, there are schematics for it. There will be a button you can push to have it addressed. By my mother. In a variety of accents.

4

Olivia Doherty achieves immortality was one of the magazine headlines. I'd bet a chainmail rhinestone-studded belt and a nude bodysuit from my eventual inheritance that Anthony thought those words were his idea. She'd only given a generalized, albeit magical-sounding description of her vision for the installation; he predicted, knowing her body of work, that it would be *breathtaking and honest.*

I wasn't sleeping. Every time I chopped vegetables for soup, I sliced open a different finger. My balance was off; I had bruises on my thighs from walking into side tables. One Wednesday after work, the slow-closing hinge on our screen door broke as I walked through it. The door slammed me in the ass, scraped my shin. I dropped my purse and cursed.

"Mom," I called. "Mom! I cannot —"

She floated into the kitchen in a whispery grey dress and handed me the phone. It was the curator from the museum, wanting to talk about unveiling the project. "I mean, we can't set an absolute date, of course," the woman said. "It all depends —"

"On when my mother dies? Because the opening has to be soon enough to take advantage of the height of the tragedy, but not so close that it's in bad taste?" I held the phone away from my ear and throttled it with both hands.

My mother sighed and plucked it from my fingers. "It's difficult for them," she said to the curator. "I'll talk to her. They'll be ready when it finally happens."

As she hung up, I said, "Mom, I can't do this. I need —"

The doorbell rang. Tom, with long rolls of paper under his arm. "I've got the AV all figured out," he told my mother, kissing her cheek and unfurling the plans across the kitchen table. As my mother leaned over them, I weighted down the curling edges with egg-shaped salt and pepper shakers sporting bird claw feet. The design looked like a spaceship built for one or two people — one of those mini-ships the geeks on Star Trek used to travel short distances when their magic beam-me-up pad wasn't working. My mother clicked the remote for her iPod and Amy

5

Winehouse filled the room. I adjusted the pepper bird foot and left.

I filed paperwork as my mother accumulated it for the arts board report and transferred the information into a spreadsheet. She does great documentation — letters, project summaries, photos, invoices. Grant reports are serious business, making sure you've checked all the boxes so they don't come back asking for a partial refund of their thirty grand. This one isn't due for a year, so if they're not satisfied, they'll have to take their refund from her estate in spiked feather boas, wigs, and dance costumes. They have such a hard-on for this project they'd probably write the whole thing off without a final report, but my mother is a stickler for doing things right. Artistically, anyway.

"Darling, listen," she said to me. "Which is the better read? 'I *know* I wasn't the perfect mother, but I always loved you.' Or, 'I know I wasn't the perfect mother, but I always *loved* you.'"

I called my brother. I said to his voicemail, "Derek, you have got to help me out here."

In the background, she crooned into her state-of-the-art microphone. She tried it with a hitch in her voice, then muttered, "Too much." Pause. "I know — I wasn't the perfect mother, but I *always* loved you."

I called Derek's voicemail again. "Derek, you have *got* to help me out here," I said. "Or maybe this read will get your attention: Derek, you have got to *help* me."

Derek doesn't find me funny. He didn't call back.

My mother has been described in any number of ways. Intelligent and strong. Lithe and beautiful. She's done nude performances. She's been shocking and bold and feminist. Inquiring and thoughtful. She's been explained to us — her public — ad nauseum.

After the initial interviews in which she revealed her impending death and gave tantalizing hints about her new and final project, my mother announced her decision to stop making public appearances. And her refusal to do chemo or radiation.

She did this through social media channels; she said she needed her wits about her for this, the most important project of her life. Her announcements were reported on TV and radio, in newspapers and online arts magazines, by journalists now used to pulling their stories from Twitter. They did their segments without quotes from her, combing through the flood of online commentary for the heartfelt and succinct, the poetic, and the clever. People ate it up, spoke reverently about her inimitable courage.

"I'm doing this for you and Derek," she said, smoothing her hand over mine, her fingers playing with the Band-Aid on my little finger. "I'm not afraid to die, but I can't bear the thought of abandoning you. With this installation, I'll stay with you forever."

The phone rang, and she leapt for it. "Yes, yes — this needs to be perfectly interactive," she said. "My words and images are for those who loved me, once I'm dead, but they're also a stand-in for everyone else's dead. And I want people to be able to take away these conversations — they need to be able to record themselves speaking to their dead."

Olivia Doherty hated euphemisms. She refused to employ softer words for death, dead, and dying.

"Dead. Dying. DY-ing. Death," she chanted into her microphone. "Dead as a doorknob. Dead as hair. Dead as a limp, bloodied skunk on the side of the road. I'm dead now. The voice you are hearing is the voice of a dead woman."

I left the house and got angry-drunk with my friend Karen, something I'd been doing more and more.

"Camille, you need to come to terms with this," my mother said the next morning, as she poured me a tomato juice and a big mug of creamy, sugary coffee. "I'm going to die, and you need to face it."

She rubbed my shoulders, her long fingers digging deep, then smoothing out the aches. I sat there seething. Also blinking back tears. But I sat there. My mother got rid of knots in shoulders like nobody else. "Ironic," I said later to Derek's voicemail. "Since she's the one who puts them there."

On hangover mornings, I'd put in earphones and find some desperately bad gothic playlist on YouTube, turn it up loud. Then I'd creep my mother on Facebook and Twitter. She didn't post often, and then only about her work, but her fans were all over those pages, pouring out their grief, their admiration, and their home remedies to cure cancer. One woman wrote that she felt closer to my mother than she did to her own mother. Some cute shaggy-haired guy wearing a washed-out grey T-shirt and faded jeans with a hole in the thigh posted a link to a YouTube video where he'd recorded himself singing a song he'd written for Olivia Doherty. Other than a few obvious rhymes, it was surprisingly good. He got thousands of hits on YouTube, hundreds of shares on Facebook. He was probably ten years older than me, ten years younger than my mother. The type of guy my mother would've had discreet sex with, if she wasn't so busy making death art.

I stumbled into the kitchen looking for more coffee. My mother was on the phone, as usual. "Thanks, sweetheart," she said. "I'll talk to you tomorrow."

I filled my mug, added heaping teaspoons of sugar and creamer, and settled on a stool at the island. The thick, oily coffee coated my furry morning teeth; as I drank, I leafed through the stack of mail on the counter. I pushed the ones that looked like cards across the island to my mother. "Was that Tom?"

"No, it was Derek."

"Derek finally deigned to call?"

"Derek calls or comes by every day. He took me to my appointment yesterday."

My throat tightened, and I set my mug on the counter; I couldn't have spoken even if I'd been able to think what to say. My mother selected a blue envelope, slid her French-tipped thumbnail under the seal. She removed a white card with blue doves and lilies on the front.

"How sweet," she said, pulling open a drawer and placing the card inside it. She reached for a stack of performance images and head shots sitting on the counter and fanned them out, frowning.

I unclenched my hands, ran my thumb over the wrinkled Band-Aid on my ring finger. "Do you think — do you really think you can anticipate — that you can control — our responses to your death? Through this monument to yourself?"

She laughed. "Monument? How ridiculous." She pulled out a shot of herself stretched athletically in an elongated sort of tree pose, naked and painted with black and green vines. She studied it critically. "I'm giving you tools. You won't know how much you'll need them until after I'm dead."

"It's kind of like you already are dead," I said, fighting down the heat flashing up through my esophagus, trying to keep my breathing steady. I looked at her muscled arms in the photograph, the way the leaves encircled her shoulders and reached for her breasts. She still didn't look very different from the photo.

"What do you think? This one?"

"Absolutely," I said. "You naked is a crowd fave." The pressure in my chest threatened to explode from my mouth in a stream of hot bile.

She tossed the photos on the table. "What do you need from me, Camille? Do you want to hear me say I'm sorry for not dying the way you need me to? For not being a better mother? Well, I am sorry. But I love you."

"I know," I said. "I hear you rehearsing those words every day. I think you've done better reads."

"Spill it, Camille," she said. "I know you don't understand what I'm doing with Exit Interview, but someday I hope you will. In the meantime, let's get on with it. Tell me what you need."

I ran the beaded ends of her turquoise shawl through my fingers, poked at the tumble of photos of her, so bold and thoughtful, so strong and lithe. Everyone was talking, all the time — the shaggy songwriter dude, strangers on social media,

9

poets, actors, journalists. The draft exhibition statement the museum woman delivered with pride last week. So many eloquent words from strangers, acquaintances, and friends. So many stupid words, too, filled with clichés and assumptions of intimacy. The world had been flooded with words of all shapes and sizes and meanings and levels of floridity.

"I'm afraid of being a bad actor," I said. "Everything has already been said — better than I could, or so melodramatically it makes me want to puke. I can't find a fresh delivery. It all feels like one of those 'triumph of the human spirit' movies we hate so much."

My mother nodded but didn't speak. She really did have an excellent sense of timing.

"Never mind," I said. "Do you want some peppermint tea?"

She nodded again. "Please. It helps with the nausea from the steroids."

"Okay." I grabbed the kettle, emptied it in the sink and filled it with fresh water. "Maybe I'll talk to you when you're dead," I said over my shoulder, "When I've had time to practise different fucking reads."

I opened the cupboard above the sink and took down a ceramic daisy-festooned tea mug, keeping my back to her. "I'll *talk* to you when you're dead," I said. I tried it with a John Wayne drawl: "I'll talk to *you* when you're dead." I fished a peppermint tea bag from a tin, dropped it in the mug and shouted, "I'll talk to you when you're *dead!*"

I heard her laugh behind me as the kettle began to shriek, but I didn't turn around.

The brilliant save

We screech around the corner in Brad's battered Mustang; he brakes hard and laughs as we slam forward against our seatbelts. We swear at him, loosen the belts from our shoulders and waists. He cranks the volume on Arsenic Machine to drown us out, but turns it down again when we remind him Zoë's mother likes to come out and give us shit for being loud.

Zoë is sitting on the steps, flexing her bare feet, admiring her toenails. The wind whips her hair around her face. She shoves on her flip-flops, unfolds herself from the step, walks to the car. She tucks her hair behind her ears, leans in and sniffs Brad's breath. "I told my mom you wouldn't be drinking."

We laugh, Brad gets out and flips the seat forward, waves Tammy out so Zoë can pile into the back with us. Her toenails are black, with sparkly silver stick-ons. Brad honks the horn.

"Move it, Jay!"

Zoë's mom comes out to the porch. "Please don't honk, Brad. You're disturbing the neighbours."

Brad leans on the roof of the Mustang, grins. "Sorry, Mrs. Johnson."

She waves, and we wave back.

"He could drive on the lawn, and she'd still smile at him," Zoë says. "She loves jocks."

Jerome bounces down the steps and slides into the front seat beside Tammy. "You got the beer?"

"Yeah, and a bottle of tequila." Brad glances in the rearview mirror, his long red hair flopping in his eyes.

Zoë smiles, like he's only looking at her.

Tammy giggles. "I can't drink tequila. It makes my mouth fuzzy."

We laugh, say at least it doesn't affect her brain.

"Hey, be nice to Tammy," Jerome says. He likes Tammy. That's why she and Zoë have been invited to hang out with us, why Tammy gets the front seat. And we know Zoë's glad to tag along. She was watching Brad all season — hard not to, to be honest, the way his crazy long hair shone red down the back of his black home game uniform. Brad's the wildest goalie we've seen. He throws himself at everything — pucks, sticks, other players. He got more penalties this year than most goalies rack up in a career.

Brad guns the engine, lays a patch of rubber. When he takes the corner, Zoë slides, and we pile against each other, too many of us now for seatbelts. She pushes herself upright again, and the car shimmies as Brad overcorrects. We all laugh. She and Brad laugh the loudest.

We drive to the coulees, music blaring, and park next to five other vehicles. We skitter down the hill toward the group, toward the river, the wind dropping as we get below the lip of the coulee. Brad leads the way, one arm in the air, a cooler under the other.

The fire is high and crackling, nested in the pit that's been sitting on this patch of silt and grass for who knows how long, built by people who used to be like us but are long gone, who fled this town to bigger and better things. The firepit is set yards away from the wide, shallow river, ringed with three layers of dusty brick. Behind us, the bushes lead into scraggly old pine trees, wound through with well-worn paths. Someone has put their iPod and a speaker on the picnic table next to an electric lantern and a bunch of beer coolers. A trance mix flickers in time with the yellow and orange flames.

A few girls from Zoë and Tammy's class cluster at the fire. They wave, but make no move toward each other. The Grade 11 girls who come to the pre-grad parties usually stick close to the guys who brought them, only finding each other when they have to stumble through the dark bushes to pee behind trees.

Brad opens his cooler, tosses beers around. We twist off the caps. Some of us lick the foaming beer from the lips of the bottles, others blow it off, laughing if it hits someone. Zoë blows at her foam, but it wobbles and stays put. She puts her mouth over it and drinks; she makes a face, then drinks again. Tammy slides up to Jerome. Zoë steps closer to the fire, tosses her beer cap into the flames. She sliced her finger on the serrated cap when she opened the beer. She puts her finger in her mouth, watches Brad.

He drinks half his beer before grabbing the twenty-six of tequila from the cooler. He throws the cap toward the river, and we hear it clank against the rocks. He swigs from the bottle, passes it around. We take deep gulps, pass it on. Zoë tips it up and fills her mouth, doesn't swallow right away. Then she does, and her eyes tear up. She blinks them away, fast. The wind shifts, she disappears inside the smoke, it changes direction again, and she's back.

"It was a great season," she says.

Brad hoists his beer at her.

"You're a crazy fucker," Jerome says. He takes a swig of tequila and offers it to Tammy. She shudders and waves him away. Brad takes it back, drinks tequila with one hand, beer with the other, passes the tequila on to us.

He really is a crazy fucker. Between the fights, the dives he took, and the vicious slap shots he loves to throw himself in front of, we figure Brad must've been black and blue all season, even with his padding. The rest of us know enough to get out of the way of something that hard and fast, survival instinct. But goalies, it's like they reverse the whole process, beat down every natural instinct. Teaching yourself not to duck? To jump toward the puck instead, when it's coming for you at seventy miles an hour? We tell him it's made him twisted.

"I'm your last line of defense, man." Brad flings his empty beer bottle into the fire; it smashes and hisses against the bricks. "Me against the shooter, me against the puck."

He grabs the tequila from us, jumps up on the bricks surrounding the firepit, straddles the flames. Jerome picks up a rock and lobs it underhand toward the fire. Brad bats it away with his free hand. We all cheer and start feeling around our feet for rocks, moving away from the fire, closer to the river, grabbing the round, grey stones that edge it. We shout and jump back as ducks burst up out of the scrubby bushes and weeds along the river. They squawk and circle in the air above us before settling back on the water, beating at the black, rippling surface. We fill our pockets, our hands, with stones; we break our fingernails scrabbling them from their dried mud beds.

We take turns tossing rocks at Brad. He stands straight, deflecting some, catching and dropping others into the fire. The flames lick up around his boots. A rock hits him in the chest; he ignores it and raises the bottle to his lips. Another rock hits his arm. His face flickers into light, then shadow as the fire sparks and twines beneath him. We start to aim a little more precisely, throw the rocks a little harder, picking up our pace as the music increases its tempo. He is hit in the chest, in the thigh, again in the chest, his free arm windmilling. The rocks fall away, clatter on the bricks, bounce into the grass. More rocks, multiple strikes to his legs and torso; one catches his cheek, opens a thin trail of red that he brushes away. Our cries drown out everything but the underlying thumping beat of the music. Tequila runs from the corners of his mouth, silvery snail trails catching the light. He drinks again, a rock hits his belly, and another; he shakes his head, his hair gold and copper snakes. He plucks a rock from the air beside his head, holds it up in his fist, then tosses it into the brush and jumps down.

"The brilliant save," he yells. We can feel the heat from his pant legs as he brushes past us and walks to Zoë. He puts his arm around her. "Never flinch. Throw yourself at it."

She tosses her beer bottle into the grass, takes the tequila from him and drinks. This time she doesn't gag. Her hand has been closed around a rock she didn't throw. She slides it into her jeans pocket.

He asks what time she has to be home, and she tosses her hair. We are all panting audibly; we unclench our fists, drop the last dusty stones to the ground. Our throats are dry and smoky, and we pour beer down them, gulping and looking for more.

"It doesn't matter," she says. "My parents won't notice."

Brad tilts her head back, pours a trickle of tequila down her throat. She swallows, wipes the corners of her eyes. He tucks a strand of hair behind his ear and lifts the bottle to his own mouth. When we yell at him, he passes it around the circle again.

Zoë turns to the cooler and starts pulling out more beer, twisting off the caps and throwing them into the fire. She passes them to us; when she hands Brad his bottle, she slips her hand into her pocket. She holds out her fist, opens it to show him. "I spared you."

Brad takes the stone from her, puts it in his own pocket. He walks Zoë away from the fire, his hand on her back, steering her down the dim path through the bushes and to the edge of the trees.

They fade to black silhouettes, the moon picking out their distinct edges then melding them into one as Brad pushes her up against a tree. She laughs. The smoke from the campfire swirls as the wind changes direction, makes our eyes water. Some ducks flap against the water again and honk to each other.

We pass the tequila back and forth. It's almost gone.

Zoë and Brad fall, tangled in foliage. Their bottles clank together and there is laughter again, the rustling and cracking of wood, then nothing but the electronic music and our own voices calling over the snapping of the fire. One thin, high shriek — why do girls laugh like that? — and the bushes start to shudder. We all cheer, except Jerome, who is kissing Tammy on the dark side of the picnic bench. Our circle around the fire is louder but smaller now. The other girls from Zoë's class are gone.

A black shape emerges from the trees again, morphs into the two of them. Zoë has her arm around Brad as they stumble through the shorter brush. He groans and stops, leans over to retch. Zoë keeps holding him up, but she pulls her body back, turns her face away while he pukes. He looks up at her, mutters something, shakes his head.

She brings him back to us, deposits him on the bench near Jerome. She is careful not to let his hair brush against her as she sets him down. Silver tears glint on his face in the moonlight. His breath is rank and sour. There is a trail of vomit in his hair, on the side Zoë'd been touching.

She pokes Jerome. "Your friend needs help. I'm leaving."

The wind whips the smoke around Brad; he fades in and out of our view.

Zoë turns away. She has a piece of stringy grey-green lichen in her hair; when we point it out, she yanks it hard, taking some hair with it, tosses the strands in the fire where they flare and sizzle.

Jerome flips her the bird. "I'm not ready to go."

"I'll walk."

It's only a mile to her house. She climbs up the bank of the coulee, grabbing at brush and weed clumps for leverage. At the top, she becomes a black shape cast on a flat world, a stick figure against the massive blue-black skyline, hair streaming behind her. Headlights loom in the distance, and she stops, waits as the car flashes down the road, its engine dropping into a deeper hum as the driver shifts gears. She coughs from the dust she's kicking up, stoops over as if she's picking rocks out of her flip-flops, straightens and walks out of sight, past our parked cars and toward the road.

When we leave, we pile into the Mustang, Brad sprawled across our legs. When we get to his house, we lay him on the doorstep, ring the doorbell, and toss the keys in the mailbox. The next morning our mouths taste dry and smoky. Some of us find rocks in our pockets. Our clothes are chalky with dried river mud.

Zoë doesn't come to parties anymore. If she's sitting on the porch when we pick Jerome up, she ducks into the house, stares at her phone or gets busy with her nail polish. Brad guns the engine as we pull away, same as always. When she hears us in the halls at school, she puts her head down or turns in a different direction. It makes us laugh, though we don't usually meet one another's eyes. We feel sorry for her, but irritated, too, at the way she hangs her head when she sees us, like a kicked dog.

Jay has a few tense weeks when Tammy thinks she's pregnant and expects him to skip parties to sit at home and hold her hand. Turns out she's not knocked up after all, so Jay's back before we know it. Tammy, when she can find another ride to the parties, stays on the opposite side of the fire, laughing too loudly.

Fucking Grade 11 kids, we say. They're not ready to play with the big dogs.

We move into the countdown to final exams, to summer. Everyone's full of plans — real plans and bullshit schemes: graduation, decamping, hockey dreams, oilfield dreams, more school. Moving on from this town. We look around and measure those of us who'll still be here in five years, hanging out at coulee parties, buying booze for underage girls.

The Saturday before grad, we peel away from Zoë and Jerome's house and back to the coulees. And that night, another car looms out of the blackness. We've just climbed back up the soft, dusty bank and stepped into the flat area where we park when this big black Buick roars by. It veers off the road toward where we're standing, just as Brad staggers on foot out of the ditch. The paramedics said he must've died instantly. We tell the story again and again in a jumble of noise that lasts for days — to the cops, the paramedics, our parents, the teachers — how the car was speeding, how Brad didn't have a chance, wouldn't have been able to get out of the way.

The principal calls an assembly, brings in a grief counselor. The driver gets a court date for long after most of us will be graduated and gone. At Brad's funeral, weeping girls lay flowers on his casket, hug each other. Tammy is among them, Zoë isn't. The teachers and coaches cry in front of us, too. They talk about tragic waste, about freak accidents, about making the driver pay.

None of us go to the grief counselor, but gradually, a bunch of stuff piles up at the top of the coulee where he was hit. Teddy bears, cards, mostly crap. A miniature plastic hockey stick, a couple of nicked pucks, the usual grocery-store flower bouquets that wilt and dry out, their plastic covers rattling in the wind that comes off that flat stretch of land above the river.

They're mounting his home jersey in a glass case at the school, and his parents are doing the same thing with his away jersey, for their rec room or something. We steal a goalie stick from the equipment room and take it out to the coulees. We slide down the bank to the firepit, break it up into a couple of pieces and douse it with starter fluid. We drink beer and tequila while it burns.

When we get back to the top, we poke through the shrine, jeering at the teddy bears. Their fur is patchy and grey with dust from the dried river mud that gets spun up to blanket the area; they are clumped and tattered from nights of rain and the constant wind, probably full of bugs.

The drawing is tucked in at the base of the shrine, so we almost miss it. It's held down by a large, smooth river rock. It's of Brad, done in watercolour and coloured pencils. The paper is already curling at the edges and warping from a few nights outdoors. The car's headlights flicker and dance around him like flames, washes of yellow and gold billowing behind him as he flies through the air. He is fixed in position, refusing all natural instinct, arms windmilling in long, graceful lines, his mouth open in a yell we can't hear. His copper hair is sticky and wet, barely gleaming, barely moving as he travels forever through space, the soles of his boots glowing brilliant orange, faint silver trails tracing his open, ecstatic face, exactly the way we remember it happening.

Coprophagy and other party tricks

Two glasses of wine on little sleep, plus Saturday night, plus adult conversation: it went to Sharon's head. She accepted a third glass and said what she was thinking.

"The doctor says there's nothing wrong. He's clean and he's fed, but he cries constantly unless I'm walking him up and down and around the house." She swirls her Merlot and rolls her shoulders. "Sometimes I can understand how people shake babies."

Rachel had been making sympathetic noises. Once Sharon dropped this stone onto the linen tablecloth, though, her mouth became a thin line.

"Come on," Sharon said. "I'd never do it, but months of no sleep topped with hours of nonstop screaming — it's enough to make anyone crazy. Let's be honest."

Rachel's husband Jeff toyed with the pieces of fat he'd spent half the meal cutting from his steak.

Allan cleared his throat and covered Sharon's hand with his. He squeezed her fingers, then picked up his fork again, seemingly engrossed in his plate.

Sharon poked at the remnants of her salad. "This would've killed in Vegas." She separated the arugula from the purple cabbage and slid it across the pool of raspberry vinaigrette, tracing a figure eight pattern over the fine green vines on the china.

"We know you're tired." Rachel pushed back her chair and began clearing plates. "Who's ready for dessert?"

Allan leapt to his feet, the ever-helpful guest, and followed her into the kitchen with the rest of the plates.

Jeff and Sharon sat in silence. Finally, she said, "So, Jeff, tell me more about that herb garden of yours."

When Sharon got pregnant, her sister cried with joy and said motherhood was the most important work she would ever do. Rachel told her she would finally know real love. Sharon heard similar sentiments from a lot of women and read more of them on the mommy blogs her friends, neighbours — strangers in the grocery store — directed her to. When Sharon said she was pretty sure she'd experienced real love before the baby came along, they laughed and shook their heads. And who was she, the new-to-the-party, not-quite-a-mother-yet, to argue? There seemed to be a couple of camps when it came to motherhood: either you claimed to love every moment, even those dark times in the middle of the night when you were crying as hard as the baby, or you posted your madcap failures on social media and got high fived for your honesty. The camps overlapped in their insistence that the whole mess was worth it.

"I hope you didn't apologize for me," Sharon said in the car.

Allan sighed. "I didn't apologize for you. I just said again how tired you are."

"That's an apology."

"Give me a break. I was just trying to smooth things over."

"At least while you scampered off to the kitchen to make excuses for me, I got to learn how to grow organic sassafras. That'll be a fun project, since I'm up all night anyway."

Allan drove the sitter home. Sharon tiptoed into Dylan's room. She watched the soft blue alligator on his sleeper move up and down with his breath. His mouth pursed and relaxed again. She turned her head away so her breath wouldn't touch his face and wake him, whispered to the air above his crib mobile, "I didn't mean it." She checked the baby monitor and backed out.

Alexander was lying in the hallway, his muzzle flat on the floor, staring into some distance she couldn't see. He didn't move his head as she approached, though his eyebrows twitched, and his eyes followed her. She leaned over to scratch his back, then his belly when he rolled over to expose it. She ran her fingers through the long silky fur on his stomach, then nudged him back to his stomach and eased his hind legs under him. He heaved himself to his feet and followed Sharon to the back door. He stumbled on the step from the deck to the grass.

"Come on, old boy," she whispered. He was deaf, but she continued to speak to him, her voice guiding him through the darkness to the tree he would pee under. When you've lived with a dog for fifteen years, a string hums in the air between you. Either one of you can pluck at it and reach the other.

In bed she said, "People used to like it when I was blunt."

Allan rolled over to face her, rubbed his forehead. "You go too far. It makes people uncomfortable."

Sharon should have been clutching at every minute of sleep, but instead she ran through other parties, the times she'd made people laugh by pushing through the unsaid. People called her brave, and honest. This was the first time Allan had said she'd gone too far, and she hadn't even been looking for a laugh. She'd really wanted to know she wasn't the only person who felt so frustrated.

Allan slid across the bed and put his arms around her. When he put his hand under her nightgown she pushed it away. "You're going too far. It's making me uncomfortable."

Allan laughed. "Smart ass." He kissed her and rolled away.

When Dylan began to cry two hours later, Sharon sat up before Allan could. "I'll get him."

"It's my turn."

"I was already awake." She groped for her robe and pulled it on, feeling her way along the wall, to the dim light of the hallway.

Dylan's fists were flailing. His mouth was distended in a howl, his face purple even in the dark. She pulled her thin robe closed and tied the belt, picked him up and nestled him against the familiar stained and re-stained patches on her shoulder. His tiny hand struck at her chin, then again. He stiffened against her, arched away. She circled the room, bounced him up and down, up and down. His cries softened but didn't stop. She kept walking, felt the ache settle deep in the muscles of her lower back.

"Fuck the fuck off, little baby. Fuck the fuck off right now. Fuck the fuck off, little baby, poor boy, you're bound to . . . Poor boy, you make me cry."

What would Rachel think if she could hear Sharon singing to her baby right now, in her sweetest, most soothing voice?

She walked him forever, in the vacuum of the night, up and down, up and down, a thousand tiny laps of the room before he nestled in, became pliant and limp against her. She lowered herself into the rocking chair, biting the inside of her mouth to keep from groaning at the pain-relief of settling her back against the quilted cushion. Dylan jolted awake several times, she rocked him and whispered the countdown: "Just ten more minutes to REM sleep, that's all, there we go, just seven more minutes and you'll be fast asleep, we can do this."

Eventually he subsided into a deep sleep, fingers falling slack against the opening of her robe. She eased herself out of the chair and lowered him over the crib, her back muscles tightening again in protest. She removed her warmth from him in increments, watching his face, holding her breath. His eyelashes fluttered, but he stayed asleep.

Alexander heaved himself to his feet when she crept out of Dylan's room. She lay down beside him in the hallway, her lower back settling against the unforgiving floor. Alexander leaned over her, sniffing at her mouth, her eyes, soft puffs of dog breath trailing across her face. The long hairs of his muzzle tickled her; she laughed, but quietly, so she wouldn't wake the monster in one room, or the man who thought she went too far in the other. Alexander sank to the floor beside her, and she scratched her fingers through the curls on his thigh as dull light patterns shifted across the ceiling.

Sunday afternoon, Sharon took Alexander and Dylan for a walk. It started to snow, but she kept going around the block, a second, then a third time, lining the stroller wheels into their previous tracks. Had she read somewhere that cold air would make the baby sleep better? Or was that just one more baby lie flooding the world? Alexander limped, favouring his left hind leg.

Back in the yard, she let him off his leash, and he plodded to his tree. She lifted Dylan from the stroller and banged at the doorbell with her elbow.

Allan came to the door, arms outstretched. The smell of his signature chili wafted out around him: beef, hot sausage, dark spices, and beer. "How's my boy? Did Mommy take you for a nice walk?"

Sharon walked back to the stroller. As she fished around for the plastic ring in seven shades of blue that Dylan liked to clutch, she looked for Alexander. The snow was already covering the grimy remnants of the last melt; a sticky blanket perfect for snowballs. Alexander had buried his nose in a drift, snuffling.

Sharon shoved through the snow toward him. She had found him eating dead birds a few times over the years, those brittle little bones such a danger to soft dog interiors. He didn't look up, even when she put her hand on his back. She nudged his muzzle with her boot.

"What've you got there, old boy?"

He continued to root in the snow, his jaws grinding. She put her hand to his mouth, snapped her fingers. He released his grip; something damp and warm dropped into her hand and she looked at what she held.

My god, he was eating shit. He had dug out a piece of his own frozen shit. A big chunk, clearly solid even before it froze; cylindrical, and stubbled with sunflower shells and tiny yellow seeds he'd scavenged from below the bird feeder. The snow around the excavation point was speckled with brown, tiny thawing flakes of shit that had — what? — fallen from her dog's muzzle? Sharon stepped back, wobbled on an uneven patch of snow. She threw the chunk over the fence into the alley.

She tugged at his collar. "Come on, old man."

Alexander obediently turned toward the house, plodded through the snow, stood waiting at the door. She kicked snow over the area then wiped her boots in a fresh drift. She bent over, grabbing snow and scrubbing her hands with it, dropping it again. Trace flakes of brown flicked through it, and she kicked the snow again. Her fingers were red, tingling.

Dylan was fussing. Allan bounced him against his chest. "I'm going to give him a bottle. What are you doing out there?"

"Just wiping the dog's feet." She picked up the old towel they used on Alexander after walks and went outside again.

She stroked her dog's back, scratched behind his ears. His head hung low, eyes focused beyond the wooden slats of the deck. Her hands shook as she swiped at his muzzle with the towel, pulled it up to examine it for shit flakes. What did it mean? Alexander had never eaten shit. She knew some dogs did. But not Alexander, not her beautiful old dog.

She was wiping too hard; Alexander gave a muted yelp. His warm bulk shifted to lean against her legs, and that was enough, finally, to make her stop and toss the towel down. She couldn't tell if his muzzle was clean. His coat was fading red, peppered with white — the perfect camouflage for hiding flecks of birdseed. She lifted his head, looked into his clouded eyes until she felt the tenuous hum of the string. She let him in the house and gave him a handful of milk bones.

Sharon washed her hands and sat on the couch waiting for Allan to finish feeding the baby. Alexander crunched through his snack and padded into the room. He eased himself into a sitting position and leaned against her knee. She ran her hand up and down his silky ear. She hated everyone in the world except her dog.

Allan returned with the baby on his shoulder.

"Somebody was supposed to tell me I'm not an evil person," she said.

"What?"

"Last night. Someone, either another mother or my own husband, was supposed to tell me I'm human, not evil, for wanting to scream sometimes when the kid won't shut up."

"Sharon, you talked about shaking babies. That's a little more serious than saying the crying drives you crazy."

"I said I wouldn't do it. Just that I understand how it could happen."

He told her that she wasn't evil. He even laughed, but it was too late. She didn't believe him. Her voice had been cold, and he'd winced when she said 'the kid' instead of the baby's name. She leaned forward, hands on her knees, elbows out, stared hard at his eyes.

"Women talk like pushing a squalling mass out of your vagina magically changes you into a different person. Maybe it does, but who the fuck says it's always a better person? What's wrong with being honest?"

"There's such a thing as too honest, including calling your child a 'squalling mass.' Maybe you've found the one subject that can't be used as one of your party tricks."

Sharon stood, felt Alexander shift as his support was abruptly removed. She slowed her rise, helped him slide to a prone position, then strode from the room. Allan used to love her willingness to confront what was unpalatable head on. He called her brave and independent. Now he was reducing that — a quality she had honed and practised under his admiring gaze — to a party trick. She had overstepped, left their friends and possibly her husband thinking she was a monster.

And her dog was eating his own shit.

At the archway between the living room and kitchen, she looked back. Dylan waved his chubby fist and gurgled. "Are you trying to punch Mommy again?" she said. Allan smiled, acknowledging her joke, so she walked back to the couch and offered Dylan her finger. His warm fingers squeezed and released, squeezed and released. A fat trail of spittle ran down his chin, and he grinned a wide, pink, toothless grin.

"Who loves their mommy?" Allan said.

Sharon wanted to roll her eyes, but she didn't. The room was tilting, and she needed to step back inside this precarious, invisible circle before she shattered it.

Dylan was charming that night, laughing and clutching at air as they dangled twirly, rattly, blue and red and yellow plastic toys above him.

"He's so perfect," Allan said.

Sharon picked Dylan up and pressed her nose into his neck. "A baby's main protection is how good it smells. Otherwise, we'd leave them in the woods for dogs to raise."

"Careful," Allan said, but he was laughing. "He can hear you."

"It's all in the tone. He doesn't know what we're saying."

Before bed she helped Alexander to his feet again. She pulled on an old black parka and followed him outside. She hadn't told Allan about the shit-eating. Every time she thought about it, her heart sped, and her breath caught, stopped in her throat, like her dog wasn't the animal she thought he was, or she wasn't the dog owner she'd imagined herself to be.

Tonight, though, he showed no interest. He pissed under the tree, and they stood together on the thin crust of snow, looking at the moon, breathing the crisp air, the overlay of exhaust. A small shape flew between the trees, visible for less than a second in the gap of streetlight. On the next block the streetlight changed from green to yellow to red.

Back in the house, Alexander settled onto his padded cushion on the hall floor; Sharon knelt and stroked his head, continued to bed.

Allan pulled her against his chest, tucked the duvet around their shoulders. She leaned into his warmth, timed her breath to the soft thump of his heart through his white T-shirt. He kissed the top of her head.

Three hours later she was up, walking Dylan. "Sweet little baby, please don't cry," she whispered. She bounced him gently, he continued to scream. She walked faster, he kept crying. She bounced him a little harder; his cry paused with the first jolt, then continued. The familiar ache spread across her lower back as she walked up and down; it expanded even as it tightened into a band of hot pain.

The moon hovered at the edge of the window, throwing pale light into the room, onto Dylan's red face. Did he feel her tension? Did it make him worse? She breathed deeply, counted, kissed his hot, wet face. The screams became a rhythmic sound that enveloped the room, twining the two of them into a cocoon where there was no time, nothing but this endless barrage of beating sound, these endless tendrils of pulsing heat sliding up her back and into her shoulders.

Eventually, she held him out from her body and looked him over: his twisted face, his flailing fists, yet another sweaty blue sleeper sporting some stupid cartoon character she didn't recognize.

"Sometimes I hate you," she said.

He pulled his legs up against his body and wailed, red with rage.

She gave him a little shake, then another. He paused his crying, she stilled herself. "You have no fucking idea," she said. "No fucking idea at all."

Her arms were so heavy. She laid him back against her chest, and he squirmed against her, still resisting. "I'm a terrible mommy," she said. "You and I know it, and now Rachel and Daddy do too."

Sharon waited until Dylan was napping the next day before taking a handful of plastic bags outside. She found a trowel in the garden shed and made her way around the yard, poking through the drifts and scooping up all the frozen, desiccated chunks of dog shit she could find. Alexander trailed behind her, seemingly unconcerned about losing this source of secondhand birdseed. She filled two bags, tied them, tossed them in the plastic garbage can on the deck, and closed the lid.

Dylan was crying when they entered the house. Sharon washed her hands at the kitchen sink, the water hot on her chilled fingers. Dylan's cries spiralled up, and she dropped the towel. Alexander lay, head flat on the floor, his clouded eyes tracking her movements. She bent over to pick up the towel, kissed his muzzle.

Changing Dylan's diaper made her gag. Unlike Alexander's firm brown chunks peppered with black and brown shells and seeds, this was runny, mustardy yellow. As she cleaned him, a thin string of shit trailed from the baby wipe, slicking warm against her hand. Eyes streaming, she tossed powder on him and bundled him up again in clean white plastic. She left him, happy now, lying on his back waving at the ceiling; she ran to the bathroom, retching, soaped her hands again and again until the water was too hot to bear.

Her life was all about shit. And then, in a small piece of her brain, way at the back, separate from the worry about Alexander, she heard herself telling the shit story at a party. The frozen ground scattered with brown spots, the hard chunk, half eaten. She would call it a 'shitsicle.' She was forming it into a story, modifying, editing; another shocking anecdote sure to elicit groans and laughter and sympathy. Maybe no one would know the name for it, but they'd all have heard of shit-eating dogs.

That afternoon, when she dangled the leash in front of Alexander, he didn't respond. She shook it a few times. He rolled his eyes up at her but didn't raise his head. She turned away to her griping child and shoved the stroller over the doorframe onto the deck. Dylan stopped, perhaps surprised by the jolt. She sped to the park, stopping twice to adjust the blanket over her son.

She made small talk with a woman she'd seen numerous times. It was funny how the park worked — the women didn't remember each other's names, just the babies' names.

"Dylan's an angel."

Sharon leaned over the stroller, brushing her finger against his cheek. The baby on the woman's lap was bald and complacent. "And Cassie's getting so big."

"Don't you usually have a dog with you?"

"He was too stiff today. He's getting old."

"That happens with dogs." The woman waved a plastic hedgehog squeaky toy at Dylan.

Dylan smiled his gummy pink smile, his plump hand clutching Sharon's finger. She shook it, then let go. She and Cassie's mother sat on the bench, jiggling their strollers.

The woman steered the talk to nursing. Sharon's nipples, formerly an inappropriate topic, were now public domain. She'd had conversations about her nipples in malls, on social media, at dinner parties, questions and stories about latching on bouncing around linen tablecloths. She went along with the subject, though her nipples were less interesting to her now than at any other time in their existence.

When she entered the house, Alexander didn't get up. She took Dylan out of his stroller, removed his blue snowsuit and knitted cap, and set him in his chair. Then she stood in the centre of the room, looking from one to the other.

Dylan waved his arms in the air. He shook his plastic rattle. When she didn't move toward him, he started to fret and pound his tray. She turned her back, went to Alexander, and lay on the floor beside him. She stretched herself out alongside him, running her hand over his head. Her free arm went around his back, scratching his spine where it had always been itchy. She couldn't remember the last time he'd wagged his tail. If the baby started to cry right then, she would lose her mind. But he did, and she didn't. She barely heard him.

"You are the love of my life," she said to Alexander. She lifted his head and turned it gently, so he was looking into her eyes. Kissed his muzzle and the space between his eyes. She whispered into each soft, floppy ear, over and over.

"You are the love of my life."

The next week, she and Allan attended a party. Not at Rachel's, this time. Sharon piled on extra eye makeup to offset the redness, poufed her hair bigger as a distraction.

A woman congratulated her on making it out to social events twice in the same month. "I found it too hard to leave Madison when she was that tiny."

Sharon didn't say that the thought of booze and adult conversation had kept her going all week. Or that the sharp stab of grief she felt on leaving her house came when she looked at her dog, not her baby.

"Didn't you ever need a break?"

"Life's too short. They'll be gone before we know it." She leaned in then, her hair brushing against Sharon's. "Don't you sometimes miss having him inside you?"

Sharon frowned; it took her a second to understand the woman wasn't talking about Allan.

She went on, "I even miss being kicked."

"Anytime I miss that, I just lean over his chair, and he punches me."

"But there was something so amazing — a communion — about being pregnant," the woman said. "It was such an intense bond, almost holy, just the two of us communicating privately."

The last swallow of wine Sharon had taken rose in her throat, lodged just below the back of her mouth in a hot rush. She uncurled her fists. "I know what you mean." Her voice was hoarse, her throat scratchy.

The woman kept talking. Sharon nodded and made sounds that would almost certainly be taken for agreement. She wasn't listening.

Her most perfect joy — her closest brush with holiness — was when Alexander used to run, all out, ahead of her, then circle back. At those moments he was all heart — purity itself — his ears streaming behind him, tongue lolling, his eyes searching for her.

The music changed to a popular song by a cheerful Hawaiian man — a song about something old going out and something new coming in. Dylan would be crawling soon, then walking; Sharon couldn't bear to think what Alexander would no longer be doing by that time.

"I hate this song," she said to no one in particular.

One of the men made a joke — wondering if motherhood had mellowed her. He was baiting her, waiting for her to tell an outrageous story. Everyone in the room paused and looked at Sharon, including Allan. He was smiling at her. They were all waiting. A woman hummed to the music, dipped a slice of cucumber in hummus. Flames dipped and rose, swaying out of time in the series of candles arranged on the fireplace mantle. A man set his empty glass against a stone coaster with a click.

Before Sharon understood the tilting, dreadful balance she had blindly, blithely engendered, she would have tossed out her story about shitsicles. She thought about diverting the conversation to her boring, newly appropriate nipples, but she couldn't do that, either.

She floundered there, trying to hear something, anything, as Allan came toward her across the room. She groped for a humming string, wondered if while she'd been standing here talking about childbirth, it had snapped permanently, was lying broken in the slush outside.

The room of pickled foods

Raymond had seen lots of fake dead people on TV, and he half
expected his grandfather to be splayed out in an unnatural
position, head lolling to the side, blood pooling beneath his ear.
He wondered if he would feel grossed out.

His mother stood at the casket in silence for a long time.
Then it was Raymond's turn. He stepped forward.

Ray Senior was lying straight, arranged in a blue suit with
his arms against his sides, nothing like on TV. Looking like his
grandfather, but also not. The weirdest detail was that he was
wearing his glasses. After Raymond had filed by, his father's
hand on his shoulder, he sat in one of the chairs, listening to the
adults. He kept sneaking looks at the coffin. He could just see his
grandfather's nose, and those glasses perched on it — not quite
straight, and set too low, so they pinched its bulbous tip.

It's not like Grandpa Ray could see anymore, so why put his
glasses on his face? Raymond turned to his father. "Why is he —"

His father shook his head, said, "Later, kid," and turned back
to the group.

Tonight was the family viewing; Uncle Ron and Aunt Erin
had dragged in a cooler filled with beer and wine; now that
everyone had made their way past the coffin and sopped up tears,
they settled in on the grey padded chairs, passing around bottles
and plastic cups.

"He was larger than life," his mother said. Her voice sounded
hoarse. "It's impossible to believe he's gone."

Raymond felt sad, but only sort of; he hadn't known his
grandfather that well, but he knew he had been a funny guy.

Raymond and his parents used to live in the same town as Raymond the first, his namesake, when he was little, but he barely remembered that. Now they lived several hundred miles away.

Twice a year Raymond's parents would pack up the car and go home to visit. The house was always full of his aunts and his uncle telling stories and drinking. Raymond was the only grandchild, so he lurked in corners listening, his grandfather at the centre of the noisy party.

"Here, buddy," Uncle Ron offered Raymond his bottle of beer. "You're what, ten? First funeral, I think you've earned a drink."

Raymond glanced at his mother. She rolled her eyes and shrugged, so he took a cautious sip. It wasn't the first time he'd tasted beer, but it was the first time he'd had permission.

Aunt Stephanie said, "If we're going to corrupt him, at least let's give him something with a bit of class." She passed him her plastic cup.

The white wine tasted sour, but Raymond took a second gulp anyway.

He hadn't been sure what to expect, but in between the crying there were outbreaks of laughter and reminiscing about Grandpa Ray's escapades.

"What a guy," Uncle Ron said, emptying his beer bottle. "Saran wrap over the toilet seat. He sure got me."

"I'd say he got us both," Aunt Erin said, "Since you staggered back to bed, and I had to clean it up in the morning."

Aunt Stephanie pointed at Raymond's father. "What about the time he piled all that snow outside your doors — the front and the back — and you were trapped in the house?"

Everyone said, "What a character," and "They don't make 'em like that anymore." And that faded their smiles; they finished their drinks and put on their jackets.

Back at the house, the adults poured more drinks, talked about the public viewing the next night and final details for the funeral the day after. Raymond curled up on the couch and listened. Occasionally, he reached for his uncle's beer bottle and took a sip. No one seemed to notice. As the stories about Ray Senior bloomed around him, he kept imagining his grandfather's booming voice, how he had made everyone laugh. Raymond stared at the wall, thinking about those glasses perched so uselessly on his grandfather's face. An idea began to grow in his mind. It stuck with him until he fell asleep to the sound of the adults still talking.

The next day Raymond poked around the house, trying to stay out of the way. He found his grandfather's trunk in the bedroom closet, where it had always been. Raymond's idea had grown all morning until he was kind of dancing with an awkward glee that would have driven the combustible adults around him mad. He hid in the TV room until it was time for his mother to nag him into dress pants and a white shirt and a blue tie. She looked past him as she put her hand on his head and called him a trouper.

He felt in his jacket pocket, fingering the plastic and wondering if he had the nerve to go through with it. He thought of his grandfather, how he was always laughing, and happiness filled up inside Raymond again. He had to do it.

Today was a larger scale version of the previous night — the official viewing for family and friends. Raymond counted forty-three people. They lined up to look at his grandfather in his coffin; the procession moved slowly as people stopped to whisper to him, even to touch his cheek or his hair, or pat his dry, waxy hands. From there they headed straight to a table holding a variety of bottles. Raymond went through the line-up again, again looking at his grandfather's blank face, those strangely pinching glasses.

The women laid out trays of snacks in the room adjoining the viewing room — pickled carrots, pickled eggs and pickled herring. People smiled at the odd assortment. "It's perfect," they said. "All Ray's favourites."

A man picked up a guitar and said, "Speaking of Ray's favourites . . ." He launched into a song about breasts and cows and milk jugs.

Raymond's mother looked at him and said, "Don't listen to this."

Ray Senior had moved an outhouse once, back on his childhood farm; in the dim evening light his younger brother Adrian had stepped into the hole. "He was still bitching about that right up until he died," the guitar player said, slapping his knee. "Kept whining how he could have broken his leg."

"That just made Dad laugh even harder," said Aunt Stephanie.

Some woman with pink lipstick said, "That man had a laugh as big as this room."

When Raymond was five, his grandfather had taken out his false teeth and held them in his hand. "I'm hungry," he said, clacking the teeth in Raymond's face, his mouth collapsing on itself as he spoke. "Feed me." Everyone had found it hilarious. Now Raymond told the story; he felt important when the adults all laughed again.

"Speaking of food, let's go enjoy some of Ray's snacks," said an old guy Raymond recognized as his grandfather's neighbour. He led the pack into the next room, saying, "Did I ever tell you about the time Ray sprayed fertilizer on my lawn in the shape of a woman's bazongas? You should've seen the wife's face when those spots grew in all bright green."

Everyone left the room. Raymond approached the coffin, looking around to make sure he was alone. Bursts of laughter came from the adjoining room. He had to tug gently to slide his grandfather's glasses off, his fingers brushing against Ray's rubbery ear. He hadn't thought what he would do with the glasses until they were in his hand; he slid them into the breast pocket of Ray's suit. Then, with a stifled giggle, Raymond pulled his grandfather's Groucho Marx glasses, complete with fake nose and moustache, from his pocket. He shook them out so the nose unflattened, and slid them on to his grandfather's face. He touched Ray's ears again as he tucked the earpieces around them; his grandfather's skin felt cool, but hard, like cement.

He stood back and grinned. This was worthy of Ray. Now all he had to do was get into the next room unnoticed. He lurked by the open door until he saw that people's backs were turned to him, then slid up to the pickled eggs, stuffing one in his mouth before moving behind his mother. He laughed loudly at the punchline to a story told by some longwinded friend of his grandfather's, as if he'd been in the room all along.

His mother glanced at him. "How many of those have you had?"

"Three," he said, grinning through a mouthful of mashed yolk.

"Those are full of vinegar. No more."

Raymond nodded. He knew he had to keep his face solemn until they noticed. His grandfather had worn the Groucho glasses every Halloween back when Raymond lived there. He used to talk in a funny voice and make the kids sing songs or tell stories. Sometimes he kept them there for ten minutes, making them earn their treats. Everyone talked about what a jokester he was. Now Raymond didn't know how long he could stand to wait for his own joke to play out.

It turned out he didn't have to wait long. His mother saw them from across the room as people headed back to the bottles to refresh their drinks.

"What the hell?" She stepped closer and Raymond started to smile. Then his mother screamed. "What the fuck is this? Who did this?" She ripped the Groucho glasses off Ray's face and waved them in the air.

There was dead silence, then the room erupted into chaos. The old fertilizer guy yelled, "What's she doing to Ray? What's going on?"

An old lady shook her head in disgust, "Such language."

"Groucho Marx, Liza, he's wearing Groucho Marx glasses."

"He's wearing whose glasses?"

"Why would the funeral director . . ."

"The kids must have . . ."

Raymond's mother screamed, "We didn't do this, you idiots." She threw the glasses across the room, her face red.

People rushed the coffin, his mother wept, his father held her, trying to quiet her sobs.

Ray was frozen in the doorway, watching people argue and mutter, explaining to each other what was happening, watching his mother cry. "She didn't have to call us idiots," the pink-lipsticked woman said in a huffy voice.

Uncle Ron retrieved Ray's real glasses and shakily put them back on his face. He moved to Aunt Stephanie, who was wailing by the drinks table.

Aunt Erin stomped over to them and refilled her glass. "It's the kind of bullshit trick he would pull," she said, glancing at the coffin with an expression that confused Raymond even more.

"Shh," Uncle Ron said, putting his hand on Aunt Erin's arm and jerking his head at the crowd of onlookers.

Raymond shrank back into the adjoining room, stuffed another pickled egg in his mouth.

His father came to find him not long afterward. "You're wise to hide. All hell's broken loose out there."

Raymond nodded dumbly, swallowed the gaggingly large lump of egg. "What happened?"

"Some jackass failed miserably at being funny, but what else is new in this family?" His father sighed. "Everyone else is gone, but I think we'll be here for a little while. Make sure you eat something."

Raymond looked at the trays of pickled foods. He wanted to puke, but he nodded.

His father walked back into the other room, grabbed a bottle of wine, and sloshed some into the women's plastic glasses. He twisted the cap off a beer and sank into a chair beside Raymond's mother. She cried and drank, drank some more, and cried.

Raymond sidled behind them and grabbed a beer, stuffing it into his pants as he escaped back to the room of pickled trays. He sat on the floor, his back to the adjoining wall, sweating. He twisted the cap off the beer and threw it at the wall. He took a sip of beer, then another one, listening to the grownups talk.

"It's the complete lack of respect that kills me," his mother said.

"Relax, Sophie," Uncle Ron said. "Erin's right. It's just the sort of crap the old man pulled on everyone else."

"It's true," Aunt Stephanie said. "And if you got upset, he'd call you a baby, say you had no sense of humour."

"Did you do it, Steph?" Raymond's mother asked. "You sound pretty pissed off."

"Christ, no," Aunt Stephanie said. "I was the victim of that shit my whole life."

"Don't look at me," Aunt Erin said. "I've had to scrub piss from bathroom walls thanks to your father. I've had to walk in it, get it all over myself peeling goddamned plastic wrap from the toilet. And that's just one of many fun stories I have. I'm with Steph. I don't do practical jokes."

Raymond was pressed against the wall, gulping the beer fast, trying not to hiccup. He was doomed. His stomach twisted in panic.

"It was disrespectful," his father said. "But you reap what you sow. I can't bring myself to get too worked up about it."

"You're right, Dad would've thought it was hilarious as long as it was done to someone else," Ray's mother said. Her voice sounded sharp, like glass. "But he would have hated having it done to him."

"Just because someone laughs all the time, it doesn't mean they have a good sense of humour," Aunt Erin said.

"The old bastard humiliated me in front of every girl I ever brought home," Uncle Ron said.

Raymond's heart banged against his chest. He held the cold beer against his face, then took another drink. He stifled a belch.

Raymond's father spoke. "That time he snowed me in, I got written up for being an hour late for work."

His mother began to sob again. "This makes me want to slap Dad as much as I want to slap the asshole who did this," she said.

There was a long silence, then, apart from the sound of his mother's shuddering breathing. Raymond could hear glasses and bottles clanking against the tabletop.

Raymond thought about his grandfather taking out his teeth and clacking them at him. Raymond had been little, and it scared him. When he shrieked, his grandfather had laughed and kept coming at him with the teeth. By the time Raymond ran from the room, he was crying. The sound of his grandfather's laughter followed him, and then his mother was holding him, stroking his hair, saying, "He's just teasing, he's just trying to be funny. He didn't mean to make you cry."

Ray peered around the corner. The adults didn't look in his direction. He could barely see the profile of his dead grandfather above the edge of the coffin, the wire of his glasses. The Groucho glasses were crumpled against the far wall. His stomach lurched. He took another fast gulp of beer. This time he did belch, a long, wet ugly sound, but no one heard him.

Gargoyle love

Shannie would like to pretend the first detail she noticed about Benedict were the shackles around his wrists. But what really arrested her were the veins in his arms — the striations in the bronze, and the faint, rough line where the sculpture mold had left raised scars on his forearms. The intimacy of the shackles, the broken chains, came later.

These arms are so different from Dominic's unveined, golden-haired arms. Dominic is unblemished, not quite eighteen years old. One of her last uses for him, she thinks, will be to help her move. School's out for the summer, and her new home is nowhere near the school where she teaches — the school Dominic attends. She has little fear they'll be seen together, and she needs the muscle.

. When they've hauled in the last boxes and stacked them behind the French doors of the dining room, she pulls two bottles of beer from the fridge and leads him up the stairs to her bedroom. "It's good luck to christen the place as soon as possible," she says. She pulls his T-shirt over his head, unzips his fly, and pushes his jeans and underwear below his slim hips. She watches him get hard as she strips. The maple tree in the back yard ripples green shadows across the blank walls.

She wraps her hand around him — her boy of the perpetual hard-on — and laughs as he pushes her back to the bed. They are done in minutes, breathing hard. He falls away from her, and she inhales a last breath of his salty smooth skin before rolling over, eyes wandering to the window, the crown moldings.

After she ushers Dominic out the door, Shannie opens
another beer. She runs her fingers over the walls and light
switches, examines window ledges, shifts from foot to foot to
learn the creaks in the hardwood floor. She'd opened all the
windows when they arrived; now the fresh air trails around her.

She's just finished the first year of her teaching contract,
and here she is, finally, in the little two-story house she's always
imagined owning — an older home in an older area, where
the porched brick infills are just starting to be snapped up by
renovating yuppies. Seniors holding out, refusing to move into
assisted living, looking out for crime, but in bed by nine. Young
couples too busy to mind anyone's business.

She steps through the sliding door to the deck. She'd closed
the deal on the house in the winter; now the grass is green, and
mystery plants have overtaken the flowerbeds. A snail trail of
sex trickles down her right leg. She lifts her bare left foot to wipe
it away, and there he is, on the top step. She'd forgotten him; he
was half covered in snow back when she bought the house. She
hadn't expected him to still be here.

A name is already forming inside her head as Shannie moves
toward the creature on her deck: Benedict. She approaches
cautiously — as if he might take flight — for, as she draws closer,
she sees the folded wings, the tautness of his arms.

She traces the sun-warmed sinews of his left arm. He is
hunched over on himself, a weary head above a scarred, muscled
body. His arms are thick and ropy — those of a manual labourer.
So unlike Dominic's bland, unaffected seventeen-year-old skin.

The sun is dipping behind the treetops, and a pair of
nuthatches creep up and down the trunk of the maple. Robins
clean the gutters of the detached brick garage. A single blue jay
screeches his creaky-gate call. The yard is aflame with colour
and sound, and rust-coloured, weathered skin. Shannie feels a
pleasant pressure between her legs as she sits next to him, still
tingling from Dominic. She rocks slightly to increase the pulse,
drinks her beer. She follows the gargoyle's gaze to the gnarled

maple tree that curves up to shade her deck and graze her bedroom window.

A professor once told her class there were two types of people who wanted to be teachers: those who'd had a successful school experience and wanted to perpetuate a system they believed in, and those who'd had a miserable school experience and wanted to change the system from the inside. Neither applies to Shannie. The scenario of half an hour before, a popular senior boy above her, his weight on his arms, panting with his need to be inside her — that was her high school experience. And Mr. Andrews, her own English teacher, for one thrilling, secretive week just after graduation. She's not about perpetuating any system, but she doesn't loathe this one, either.

She wanders her bedroom that night, smoothing the freshly made bed, reluctant to end the day. A bright moon slides into the room. Thin clouds weave across the sky, the moon gliding across them. Benedict looms on the step. Shadows flicker, and she imagines she sees a wing twitch. She lies naked across her bed covers, and the night rustles.

Dominic shows up a week later, mid-evening. Boxes and paint cans have been stowed away; the walls gleam soft yellows and greys. Art prints have been hung, and candles burn from low votives. He walks in after a perfunctory knock.

"Nice," he says. "You've done a lot." He walks the room, picking up items and setting them down again in the wrong places.

"What makes you think you can stroll in here without an invitation?"

He shrugs. "I had nothing to do. I thought you might be lonely."

Shannie stretches and runs her fingers through her long hair. "I wasn't, but I can probably find a use for you, now that you're here." She walks back to the kitchen and takes beer from the fridge. "Let's go outside." She leads him to the deck and sits on the step beside Benedict.

"What the hell is that?"

"A gargoyle."

"Why would you buy something that freaky?"

"He was here. I think it's his house." Shannie clinks her bottle against Benedict's shackles, then Dominic's beer, drinks. A crow calls from a neighbouring pine tree.

She gestures at the yard with her bottle. "I'm going to put bird feeders up, and plant bulbs in that bed in the fall."

"You sound like my mother. She's always going on about her garden."

"Maybe I have more in common with your mother than with you. Other than how much you want to take my clothes off."

"You haven't called me."

"Don't be boring," she says.

She said goodbye to Dominic in her mind the day he helped her move. He'll be off to college in the fall, and good riddance. Just one more beautiful, voracious boy. She revels in their longing — what woman wouldn't? The way they test themselves against her. But Dominic is the first student she's slept with since she was a student herself. And the last. It's time to behave like an adult.

After tonight.

Dominic broods on her left; his knee brushes hers, and she presses against it. "Stop pouting. It makes you less pretty."

He leans in to kiss her, and she pushes him away. "Not out here."

He slides his hand up her thigh, and she stands and steps into the house.

"Shut the door behind you."

He follows her in, closing the screen door. She climbs the stairs and pushes open the curtains on her wide, high bedroom window. When he tries to kiss her, she moves away from his mouth, places his hand on her breast. She pushes him back on the bed, pulls off his jeans and underwear, removes her shorts and tank top. She straddles him and sinks down. He is rippled

44

with shadows and dusk beneath her. He feels like satin, or sun-warmed bronze.

Afterward, Dominic rolls away and splays on his back, hands behind his head. "So, Ms. Langston, I've got something to tell you."

"What's that?" She trails her fingers across his warm, lean body.

"I'll be back in your class this fall."

"What?" Shannie is frozen for a long moment, then she pastes on a smile and twists lazily in his direction. "Why? You graduated."

"I'm sticking around for another year." His grin grows broader, now that he has her full attention. "I need to get my marks up. I didn't get the scholarship I wanted." He stretches. "So, I'm going to stay back, play football again, and nail the scholarship next year. Maybe I'll nail the English teacher some more while I'm at it."

Shannie forces a laugh. "Why do you need to take English 30 again?" He took and passed her class the first semester, before she started sleeping with him. A fine distinction, perhaps, but it kept certain of the worst potential complications at bay, in her own mind at least.

"Barely. Besides, I like your class. I think you're a real good teacher." He runs a lazy hand across her stomach.

Fifteen minutes later, Shannie is guiding him out the door, wearing the cool, amused mask she uses in the classroom. He swaggers down the mossy, bricked sidewalk that wends to the back alley where his bright new truck is parked, turns, salutes her. She closes the door. She wants to vomit.

She dreams of Dominic that night. He comes at her, laughing when she pushes him away. "I'm the only friend you've got," he says. His face is twisted, cruel. She wakes with a shudder. Stars flicker through the skittering branches outside her window.

The dream-Dominic is right. She'd been too busy drowning in lesson plans and marking the first semester to get to know the other teachers. And they seemed old — thickset and boring. The gym teacher, Gary, postured for her, throwing himself against the boys in lunchtime matches. Shannie would watch the lithe young bodies weave around his heavier, powerful frame. He was not sleek or beautiful.

And then Dominic walked into the trendy cocktail lounge she used to work at, holding his fake ID. On a night when her skin didn't feel like it fit properly over the new shape she was trying to take on. A night when she needed to slip back into the familiar groove of bar stools and tequila shots and flirtations.

Shannie hasn't had a vacation in years. University was followed by two years of substitute teaching, slinging drinks throughout. She's been anticipating the luxury of summer — long days of puttering in her new yard, of lounging on patio furniture with faceless laughing people, holding nameless drinks in pretty glasses, all of them gleaming in the sunshine like a magazine spread. The thrill of selecting a new lover.

Now, she can't stop working. She digs sod, creates a new flowerbed, treats the soil. She makes trips to the garden centre for perennials, arranges them in various patterns on the dirt. Anything to keep from thinking about the fall, about Dominic, how he will smirk at her in class.

Shannie rubs a dirty hand against an itch on her forehead, stretches her aching back. She moves to the deck, lands with a thud beside Benedict. Her beer is sun warmed and flat on her tongue. A white cat leaps onto the fence and saunters along it before seeing her and stopping. Its tail twitches, its eyes widen, impossibly large and green. It leaps from the fence to the alley, disappears.

Shannie shivers in the heat, goes inside and brings out another beer. Her fingernails are blackened with dirt, chipped and broken. There are no messages on her phone, but there will be soon. Dominic in control, the balance of power shifted.

Next door, a woman works in her garden. She raises a hand to Shannie, walks to the fence. "Welcome to the neighbourhood.

I'm Janet." She gestures toward the house. "My husband, Roger, is in the house."

The woman is in her mid-sixties, an avid gardener. They talk about yardwork, and then Janet says, "Some boy came over the other day when you weren't home. He knocked at the front door, then came around to your deck and looked through the door."

"That's my nephew." The woman's eyes are bright, Shannie sees. Unlikely to miss much. "He helped me move, and he does odd jobs sometimes."

"Roger recognized him." Janet laughs. "He stopped me before I called the police."

"I'm lucky I have such observant neighbours."

That night, Shannie dreams she is falling. She wakes with a jolt, heart hammering, fingers clutching at air.

When her phone rings, she checks the call display before answering. It's Gary, the gym teacher from her school. Inviting her to a barbeque at his house.

"It's time you got to know some of the other teachers better," he says. "Bring beer or wine and we'll take care of the steaks."

Shannie hesitates. But maybe it's not too late — maybe she can still step into their circle. And she might need allies.

"Yes," she says. "Yes. It sounds fun."

The air is dead tonight, the sky devoid of clouds. The solar powered lights she placed in the flowerbeds glow up the trunk of the maple. She lies awake, replaying moments of herself in the classroom — with Dominic, with all her male students. Of course, she enjoys their attention — it's flattering. But she hasn't been inappropriate in class, really. No one expects her to wear only high-necked shirts or bind her breasts. And she's been careful to keep her female students on side: if there's one scent high school girls can pick out in an instant, it's competition.

She's not looking forward to the party, not at all.

She drifts, wakes again to feel the bed shifting. It sinks, at her right hip, as if someone, in the darkness, has lowered himself to sit beside her. Her heart pounds at her chest. She tries to reach for the lamp, but she can't move. Her body wants to roll to the right, into the depression in the mattress: she is simultaneously paralyzed and holding herself rigid against falling into that low spot. The only sound in the room is the thrum of her panicked heart hammering blood through her. The feeling of a presence lingers, then begins to lift. She stares into the darkness of the room, and finally, gradually, is able to raise her head. She turns on the lamp to an empty room.

Shannie wakes depressed and groggy. She pulls on a T-shirt and shorts, stumbles down the stairs. Looks at her coffee pot. The eerie sensation she'd felt, the certainty that someone was sitting beside her on the bed, is still with her. She opens the fridge, pours tomato juice into a large glass. As an afterthought, she pulls vodka from the freezer, adds a generous shot, and takes it onto the deck.

A squirrel rushes sparrows at the bird feeder, fills his cheeks with seeds. The birds wheel away and return; the squirrel cracks open a seed and glares, tail jerking. She sits in her spot on the step beside Benedict.

"I have no friends," she says. She drinks half the Bloody Mary, leans against Benedict's hard, weather-beaten thigh. Maybe she should bring him up to her room. To protect her. His horns are warm under her fingers; she circles them at their bases, traces them to their tips and back.

The white cat leaps onto the fence, stares coolly at her, widening its luminous green eyes before jumping back down into the alley. Her neighbours are laughing, mowing their lawns, bringing in newspapers. Her neighbours have real friends who walk in through the door, who are not visitations in the dead of night.

Shannie cleans out an overgrown flowerbed until her back and knees ache. Occasionally, she goes into the house to pour herself another Bloody Mary. She makes a piece of toast in the early afternoon, sets large stones she has found at the river into the new bed. She moves slowly, dragging out her tasks.

When Dominic shows up, she wants to cry.

"Don't you have anything better to do?" she asks. "Like work?"

"Better than you? I don't think so."

Shannie straightens and turns to scan Janet's yard. She can't see anyone.

"Aren't you going to offer me a beer?"

Shannie shakes her head. "I have things to do."

"Well, there's something I want to do." He grins at her; the energy flicks off him in little bright sparks, his veiled sense of triumph. He reaches for her waist, fingers creeping up under her tank top.

Shannie bats his hand away and steps back. "Stop it. The neighbours will see." She backs further away from him, tries to smile again. "Look, this isn't a good time. I was about to get in the shower and go meet a friend."

"Who?"

She shrugs. "You don't know this person."

"Person? Is it a man?"

"That's not your business." She uses her firm classroom voice. "Go hang out with kids your own age. We've been having fun, but you know we don't have a future."

"I think we do," he says. "We have five months of hanging out in English class together. It's going to be a lot of fun, you and me keeping our little secret from everyone else in the class. In fact, it might be fun to fuck you in the classroom, on your desk."

He moves toward her again, and she glances at the neighbours' house. "Don't," she hisses. "I told you, I'm on my way out. You have to leave."

"Then take me inside where I can kiss you goodbye without anyone seeing."

Shannie's hands shake as she slides open the door and steps inside. "Don't threaten me."

"I'm not threatening you, Ms. Langston." His smile is mocking. "I just feel sad when you push me away." He slides his hand under her shirt again, kisses her. She kisses him back, lets him slide his warm fingers inside her bra, play with her nipples.

She watches him leave from the kitchen window. In the yard next door, Janet lifts a hand, and he waves at her.

Her room is stifling that night, the day's heat collecting in the rafters. Shannie tosses on top of the covers, then throws herself from the bed again to stand naked at the dark window. A faint breeze stirs the leaves outside and trails across her stomach. A sliver of moonlight glances over Benedict's wings; she blinks, and they seem to twitch. She rubs her neck and widens her stance so the breeze can slide between her legs, lick along her sticky skin.

In the night, Shannie startles awake, straining to hear, to see, in the blackness. Her skin crawls with the certainty that something is there, beside her, has been watching her sleep. She tries to turn her head; she can't move. She is filled with terror, her heart beating so fast it feels as if it's coming up her throat.

A weight descends on her chest, pinning her to the bed. She tries to struggle but her body is paralyzed, unable to form sound or draw breath or fight against the jackhammer of her heart. The weight on her chest intensifies, becomes a body on hers, pressing the length of her. She tries to move again, but her body is lead, impossibly heavy. She can feel herself being entered, split apart roughly. The room clamours with her rapid breathing, with the pounding invisible energy. She is battered relentlessly from every angle, and she can't move, can't speak — and then the presence withdraws from her again, and the room stills.

Shannie gasps. She tries to move her fingers and now she can — they twitch against the sheet. Her pulse throbs at her neck and wrists and temples and knees, and she stumbles from the bed to the doorway, flicking on the light. She huddles under her blankets in the bright room.

She wakes feeling dull, hung over, and beaten. She shoves aside the tangled sheets. The yard is bright with sunshine and birdsong. It all looks so normal. She feels drugged, like a bee on a hot summer day. Lawnmowers buzz down the block. A shiver runs through her: she touches herself, feeling for bruises that aren't there.

Shannie takes her coffee out to the deck, runs her fingers over Benedict's arm again and again, as if he were a worry egg. She drinks two mugs of coffee before throwing herself into weeding, rearranging stones. Mid-afternoon, she finally breaks to scrub her hands, make a salad, open a beer.

She lies on her back in the grass, and her muscles slowly unclench. An insect crawls along her arm. She is calmer now; she knows it was a dream. She's an educated woman with an active imagination.

Her reaction the night before was excessive — too much like the melodrama of a crazed woman in white, locked in an attic. Or a mystic — one of those women whose spiritual experiences are intensely sexual. She laughs, moves to her usual spot next to Benedict. A mystic she's not, and definitely not a saint. She plucks at his left wing, as if it might unfurl in her fingers.

She showers and dries her hair, runs through the names of the teachers she'll be seeing tonight. Their faces blur in her memory, as if she hasn't seen them in years. She puts on eyeliner and mascara, chooses capris and a yellow T-shirt.

Before leaving the house, Shannie opens the drawer that holds her neglected curriculum plans, hoping the sight will pull her back into the calm plan that used to be her life. Instead, terror rises at the thought of September. She shoves the drawer closed against it and slams out of the house.

Gary greets her at the door with an embrace she didn't expect and tries to avoid; the six-pack of Corona she carries jabs into her breast. Music and laughter drift in from the deck: Belinda, one of the science teachers, and her husband Nolan; Brett, the drama teacher, and his fiancée Tess.

These happy, dull people talk of their summer. Belinda and Nolan are avid golfers: they relate their last game in detail. Shannie admits she has never golfed.

"I'll teach you," Gary says, squeezing a slice of lime into her bottle. "You'll love it."

"I don't know if I'll have much of a life for the next few years," she says. "All that lesson planning."

They laugh in the still-hot late afternoon sun, drink beer, and tell stories about students. Shannie feels ill. What would these friendly, boring people think if they knew her student story? She forces herself to take part in the conversation, but she keeps imagining how their expressions would change, how they would look at her. Her head aches, a dull band that tightens around her forehead with each cheerful pleasantry.

Clouds begin to gather in the distance, and they move inside as the air gets heavier. Gary corners her in the kitchen. "You're just what the school needs, fresh ideas, youthful enthusiasm." He puts his hand on her arm. "I'm glad you're here."

When she doesn't pull away, his fingers stroke her inner elbow lightly. Sprinklings of dark hairs grow above his knuckles. His smile is loose, sloppy looking. She hesitates, considering, and he leans in. She holds her breath and lets him kiss her. It is as sloppy as she expected, his mouth too wide, too wet, his tongue trying to push past her lips. She kisses him back, flicks her tongue to touch his; but her stomach rolls. She pulls away and mutters her excuses, her thanks for the evening, the lovely dinner. Flushed with her response, he does his best to persuade her to stay as the other guests begin to make departure noises. Her head throbs. She avoids a second kiss and escapes to her car.

The weather has broken. She drives home through rolling thunder and enters her house just as the deluge begins. When she checks her cell phone, there is a voicemail from Dominic.

"I want to see you tomorrow. Don't make me wait until school starts again."

Shannie rubs her pounding forehead. His voice is challenging, the threat barely below the surface. The phone slithers from her damp hands as she jabs at the keypad to delete his message. Rain hammers against the roof, the windows. She climbs the stairs without turning on any lights.

She tosses her clothes to the floor, drags on an old set of flannel pyjamas. The sky is thick and low. Benedict is hazy through the rivulets racing down the glass. She closes the window and lies on her back, clutching her flannel shirt closed at the neck. The rain is a relentless patter above her. Her mind pings between images of Dominic's mouth — leering and commanding, spewing secrets — and Gary's — possible protection, but growing more grotesque, more sloppy, with each thump of her heart.

She wakes to the presence in the room. The bed shifts. She tries to speak, no sound comes out. She tries to turn her head, but can't. Then the weight on her chest again. She is breathing faster, gasping voicelessly for air. The weight pushes her deeper into the bed, spreads itself the length of her body, against her, inside her. As her breath comes quicker, the pressure builds against her, envelopes her, grinds against her helpless hips. She imagines stone fingers.

Shannie isn't sure how long it takes before she is once again able to move. Time seems to have suspended itself. The rain drizzles outside, a thinning veil against the night. She eases herself from the bed and turns on the light.

She wakes again with a jolt, another dream in which she is falling. She is curled upright in the corner of her bedroom, pillow jammed between her head and the wall, wrapped in the comforter. Grey light trickles into the room. The rain gusts against the window.

Even with the lamp on, the room is dull and cold. Shannie clutches the blanket, afraid to move. She is being punished. She will be at Dominic's mercy until he is done with her. Gary can't help her, nor can she bear that loose mouth on her body as penance. Dominic's mocking face looms before her; he will break her, just for fun. Shannie knows now — he will break her even if she continues to have sex with him. Her fingernails dig into her palms as she sits in the corner, tears pasting her sweaty hair to her cheeks. Rivulets trace jagged patterns down the window.

Dominic's face blurs, sprouts horns. There was the feeling last night of cold stone fingers. She chokes on her fear, pushes off the floor, wrapping the blanket around her. She stumbles on the stairs, grabs at the railing and swings against it, bruising her hip. Beyond the sliding glass door is Benedict's slick, gleaming back.

She lets the blanket fall, wrenches at the door. She is out on the deck in her bare feet, shoving at the gargoyle with all her strength. He shifts closer to the edge of the step, and she shoves again. He topples off the first step, crashes down the second and third and lands sideways in the flowerbed, intact. Shannie slips in a puddle, wrenches her ankle as she wrestles a large stone from a flowerbed. Holds it over her head and smashes it on Benedict with all her strength. The rock clangs against him, thuds to the sodden earth. His wing is chipped. She picks the rock up, batters at his face again and again. His horn breaks off, the rock bounces into the mud. Her hands are bleeding.

Shannie heaves the rock at the gargoyle again. It clatters away from his solidity without causing fresh damage. She pushes sodden hair from her eyes and looks around the yard, at her neighbours' houses. Is that a shadow she sees behind Janet's window, the curtain twitching?

She wipes her muddy, bloodied hands on her pyjama bottoms, stumbles up the steps. Her feet slip on the wet wood, mud-heavy pants tangling around her ankles; she crashes to the deck, pain shooting up her arms as she lands with her weight on her hands, her teeth chattering so violently she bites her tongue.

She hears a scrabbling noise, lurches upright in fright. From under her deck, the white cat emerges. Its fur is slicked and patchy from the rain, its eyes huge, baleful green in its triangle face. It stops at the sight of her, hunches, tail twitching, then slinks away, eyes on hers until it reaches the fence.

It leaps, and, with one last glare, it's gone.

A sandwich for the road, and a sketch

"Black washes Audrey out. She looked terrible." Connie removes the straw from her drink and licks the salted rim of the glass. A glob of green slush slides down the straw and lands on the table.

"To be fair, planning a funeral is exhausting," Justine says.

Phoebe is irritated that it's left to her to say, "And she did just lose her husband."

"At least she had decent food," Connie says. She licks the last slick of slush from the straw and sets it on the table. "I like those little sandwiches with the crusts cut off. Very high tea."

"I couldn't get past the egg salad and tuna," Justine says. "God knows how long they sat out." She mops up Connie's spill with a napkin, folds the abandoned straw inside it and pushes it under the tent card advertising twelve flavours of chicken wings.

Phoebe is on her third drink. She doesn't want to talk about sandwiches, and she definitely does not want to talk about Audrey, who they do not consider a friend, and who has only been part of their consciousness for two years. Connie started to cry the moment they settled at the wood-veneered pub table. They'd had to comfort and calm her and shift from Pierre's death to peripheral topics.

Phoebe drums her fingers against the base of her wineglass. Connie is also on her third drink, and regardless of the danger that may lie therein, Pierre is what they're here to talk about. She wouldn't be in a bar with these women otherwise.

"How does someone, in this age of technology, get hit by a train, anyway?"

"It happens a lot," Connie says, narrowing her eyes at Phoebe. "More than you'd think."

Justine laughs. "I'm sure it does." She drains her first glass of wine, finally, sets it on the table with a firm click. "Maybe if you live in Saskatchewan." She laughs again and shakes her head.

Connie gasps. "I just — I can't —" She gulps a mouthful of green slush; Justine pats her arm with one hand while gesturing to the waiter with the other. The music switches from hard rock to country. Phoebe bobs her head to it.

Pierre Rouillard taught art at the university — they got the news of his bizarre death only after two first-year painting classes had waited patiently for his arrival, eventually growing so absorbed in their canvases they'd forgotten his absence. The news trickled fast, through the university and beyond to Phoebe, as efficient as any small-town telephone prayer chain. And his colleagues and friends were drawn to their favourite pub like iron filings, only to witness Connie pull the same histrionics she's repeating today.

Someone said to Phoebe that night, "I know this is sad for all of you, but I especially feel for Connie. She's devastated."

"Some of us prefer to be quiet in our grief," Phoebe had said.

Pierre taught art history, drawing and painting. His medium of choice was watercolour. Phoebe found that odd; she associated watercolour with softness. But Pierre's painting was like his personality: bold in subject and colour, without the layers acrylic or oil would have invited. His paintings had vivid edges and loose centres, intriguing at first glance, although Phoebe had failed, on closer examination, to make much sense of them.

Phoebe met Pierre five years ago through her communications business. She wrote annual reports and web text, managed social media accounts for a handful of clients: cabinet companies, dog groomers, the local AIDS organization. She briefly dated a sessional art instructor who hooked her up with the university; the instructor is long gone, but the university still brings her in every semester to teach third year art students how to write artist statements.

She teaches them to avoid adjectives, not to get too esoteric in their descriptions. "Your artist statement is not about your soul, it's about opening a door between what you put on the canvas and what the viewer sees," she tells them. "Leave space for them to discover what it means to them, not what it means to you."

She runs them through exercises, comes back a week later to review and critique, then one last class to help them polish their statement for the semester's work and to review how they can apply these principles to future shows.

She and Pierre would linger after class; he'd say that she kept the students from taking themselves too seriously. She started getting invited to faculty arts parties.

Now, she turns away from Connie's swollen eyes and the Rorschach blotches of mascara seeping into the lines around them, pushes back her chair and goes to the washroom. She sits in a stall and blinks back tears. The university ad framed on the inside of the door hangs at the correct eye level for a person sitting on the toilet. It has a 'best days of your life' vibe — carefully casual models texting messages back and forth about the big game. The men have two days' worth of stubble, the women's hair is pulled into messy buns.

There were many parties, pre-Audrey; one she remembers in particular. She didn't know Pierre that well yet. He was drunk, and his shaggy black hair was greasy. Even his goatee looked greasy, the bristling zigzagging hairs in it more yellow than white. He wore a faded beige Rolling Stones T-shirt over a blue and red plaid cowboy shirt with pearl snaps at the wrists. The Stones tongue was faded to near invisibility. He smelled as though he smoked in bed and slept in his clothes.

She looked him over as she lifted her drink to her mouth. "Are you being ironic?"

He laughed.

"You cut your own hair, don't you?"

He laughed again. His hair was hacked at, a careless thick bob across the nape of his neck. She let him get a little too close, sat beside him a little too long.

She liked seeing him at parties; after they'd had a few drinks, his style did seem ironic, even vaguely romantic in its dissipation. The way his stained fingers shoved his hair aside; the way he'd laugh, then cough.

She'd asked Rob to drop her off at the funeral home, but discouraged him from attending the funeral. "You didn't know him well," she said. "I'll be fine. We're going for drinks afterward."

The reason she didn't want Rob with her is wrapped up in her purse — a remnant of another party. A memento she has been holding close these past, sorrowful days; a symbol of the unique relationship she had with Pierre, a relationship even she didn't understand until he'd died.

When she gets back to the table — assuming Connie can get hold of herself — Phoebe will pull it out and show them. Maybe after one more drink. Let the talk that Connie has been courting — tales of relationships and loss — finally unfold.

Phoebe straightens her clothes and exits the stall. As she stands at the mirror to wash her hands, she sees a bit of tuna sandwich caught in her bottom teeth. It's from more than an hour ago, when she had a nibble of sandwich at the funeral. No one has pointed this out to her, though they've surely seen it as she spoke. She pries the tuna out with a fingernail, marches back to the table. Connie is leaning in, talking urgently to Justine.

Phoebe shoves her purse strap over the arm of her chair as she yanks it out from the table. "People are so rude at funerals," she says. "They monopolize the person everyone needs to talk to, even when they see you're waiting."

She'd stood at the edge of the group surrounding Audrey for an embarrassingly long time, trying to catch her eye. The widow had been crying earlier; now she was speaking animatedly with a couple. As the conversation ebbed, Phoebe stepped forward. A man brushed past her and handed the widow a glass of orange punch. Phoebe finally pushed through and offered brief condolences before joining Justine and Connie at the door.

"When I went over, they weren't even talking about Pierre," Connie says. "They were talking about the Olympics."

"The Olympics have been over for almost a year," Justine says.

"I know," Connie says. "They were talking *theoretically*. About the *idea* of the Olympics. At her husband's funeral."

She shakes her head as the waiter arrives with three shot glasses. "Jagermeister," Connie says. "To toast Pierre. It was his favourite."

Phoebe takes a breath. "Before he quit drinking, anyway." She extends her glass. "To Pierre."

The others echo her words; they clink glasses and drink. Phoebe shudders at the dark green flavour and gulps her wine. The buttery tang of the chardonnay doesn't wash away the taste of the shot, so she drinks again, swirls the wine around in her mouth.

"Your eulogy was good," she says to Justine. "Respectful and sincere." Privately, she felt Justine had focused too much on academia, on her own importance as faculty chair. She had also addressed almost exclusively the past few years of Pierre's life, perhaps out of deference to Audrey.

Phoebe sets her glass down. "But now we can tell the stories that aren't fit for public consumption."

"The stories that go way back," Connie says. "The pre-Audrey stuff." She gestures the waiter over again. "I'll have a daiquiri this time."

Phoebe nods at her near-empty glass. Justine shakes her head and turns to Connie. "I was surprised Audrey didn't ask you to speak at the funeral, too. You've been the arts admin for — what — fifteen years? You knew him longer than all of us."

Connie huffs out air. "I knew she wouldn't." She finishes her margarita and pushes it away, looking toward the bar. "It's just as well. Why rock the boat at a funeral?"

Justine smiles. "Rock the boat?"

"She never liked me."

"I don't think Audrey liked me, either," Phoebe says. "I get the feeling she's insecure." She takes a deep breath and reaches for her purse, for the slim package it holds, the plastic and cardboard protecting the drawing inside. The waiter returns with fresh drinks, and she releases the package again, sliding her fingers across its slippery surface as she pulls her empty hand from her purse.

"Whether she acknowledges it or not, Pierre lived an entire life before Audrey came along," Connie says. "The first time he brought her to the office, he told her I was the other half of his brain, the one who kept him functioning." She sucks at her drink, smiles around the pink straw. "She was polite, but I knew she had a problem with how close we were."

"She did have a positive influence on him," Justine says. "He stopped boozing, got a haircut. He started showing up at department meetings, pulling his weight."

Phoebe leans forward, puts her elbows on the table. "I liked his hair better shaggy. And I know it was good for his health to quit drinking and smoking, but he used to be so much fun at parties. I remember —"

"That health routine was about control, about separating him from the people who loved him," Connie says. "But he still kept a few secrets."

"Secrets?" Justine is also leaning forward now, smiling. "Do tell."

"I can't talk about this —" Connie fumbles for a tissue, pushes back her chair. "I have to pee."

As Connie weaves toward the bathroom, Justine turns to Phoebe. "She thinks we think she was having an affair with Pierre."

"What?" Phoebe's hand gropes for the stem of her wineglass as she laughs. "Her? She's not remotely his type."

"Not even at his drunkest."

"I miss drunk Pierre," Phoebe says. "I liked him better when he wasn't showering. Is that wrong?" She reaches for her purse again, slips her fingers inside to touch the plastic bag. "He and I used to —"

"It was a bit pathetic at the funeral, all those women crying, thinking how Pierre was secretly in love with them," Justine says. "How they all had these secret claims on him."

"Really? Do you think?"

Justine rolls her eyes. "Pierre knew how to work women — those sad eyes, all that 'I'm a mess but you could save me' bad boy crap."

Phoebe's hand stills. "I guess, being Pierre's colleague, you see things I don't," she says. The room is filling up with the after-work crowd, and the music is louder now. Under the table, she winds her purse strap tight around her finger until she feels it swell. A blonde man carrying two pint glasses sloshes beer near her foot. He continues without looking at her, the scent of cigarette smoke trailing from his clothes. A track of beer-drops dogs his footsteps across the worn wooden floorboards to disappear behind the pool table.

Justine shrugs. "Pierre was harmless."

Phoebe says, "I have to go to the bathroom."

"If you're wise, you'll wait until Connie gets back. You don't want to be trapped for an hour in some weeping high school washroom drama."

Phoebe nods, drinks, looks around the room. The waiter weaves through the tables with a loaded tray. The blond man who'd spilled beer at her feet is chalking his pool cue, laughing with a bearded man.

Connie returns; no more Rorschach blotches. Phoebe avoids eye contact, bumps her hip against a chair as she walks through the rapidly filling tables into the bathroom and into a stall. She unzips her pants, yanks them down to her knees and sits on the toilet, her purse on her lap. She pulls out the flat package and unwraps it as she pees. It's a line drawing of her, done by Pierre four years ago. After Rob, but before Audrey.

When Rob started coming to parties with Phoebe, she'd wait until he was engrossed in conversation, then go in search of Pierre. This particular night, most people were in the kitchen. Pierre was sitting on a flowered loveseat at the far side of the adjoining living room, a near-empty glass of whiskey beside him, head bent over a piece of paper.

He tossed his pen on the coffee table and handed her the paper — dark scrawls on a white napkin, an unfinished woman with waving lines of hair, an awkward light added to the heavily lashed eyes.

"Who is this?"

"It's you," he said. His eyes were bleary and red.

She laughed and sat beside him, letting her thigh press against his. The scent of stale smoke and unwashed hair wrapped around them in their quiet corner. She held the drawing out for him to sign, then tucked it in her purse. After Rob left that night, she studied it, smiling. His signature was a drunken, looping scrawl: Pierre Rouillard. She looked at it a few times over the next day, then put it away in a drawer, along with a couple of smutty novels and some old letters from previous boyfriends.

Phoebe studies the drawing now. It isn't very good. It could have been any of a number of women with long hair, but then, he'd tossed it off drunkenly, hadn't he? With little thought, and with pity-me eyes. The way he did everything until Audrey cleaned him up.

Pierre grew a soft paunch. He wore non-ironic shirts in solid colours. His wiry hair was barbered, though never very neatly, and sometimes it still looked greasy. At parties, the four of them spoke in a friendly way — he and Audrey, she and Rob. It was less interesting to her than the drunken corner conversations she and Pierre used to share; she felt less interesting to everyone. The parties got less loud, broke up earlier. Pierre and Audrey often didn't attend.

In the ad on the stall door, the designer has used the university's corporate font in its simulated text messages. It looks ridiculous — nothing like the way text messages actually look. It makes her angry, that they would sacrifice authenticity for branding and expect no one to notice or mind. The plastic and cardboard that had protected Pierre's drawing falls from her naked knees to the floor. She leaves it there, stuffs the unprotected drawing back into her purse. The fake-happy fake-students on the poster look overwrought and manic.

Somehow, Phoebe had been imagining the old Pierre, half-drunk and unshowered, as the one struck and killed by the train. It was too clichéd, otherwise — the sort of coincidence she and that earlier Pierre would laugh about at a party — a city man in a newish car, mowed down by a train at a signalled crossing. The casket had been closed, but, in her mind, his arms were crossed casually across that stupid Stones T-shirt, his haircut choppy and self-administered. Irony and metaphor abounded. In actuality, Pierre's death had been as sloppy and casual as his art; he'd probably been wearing a golf shirt.

When she's talking to students, Phoebe tells them it's about making space where the meaning can reveal itself. She cajoles words from them — what they want from their audience, and what their audience needs from them. It always seems so clear. She grabs the plastic and cardboard wrapping from where it's fallen to the floor at her feet, shoves it into the silver tampon disposal bin on the back wall of the stall. The bin clangs shut, echoing in the empty room. She levers herself up off the toilet seat, loses her balance, drops to a sitting position again. She slides her purse to the floor and leans over to dig through it. The drawing brushes her fingers and she shoves it deeper into her purse, comes up with a second package.

At the funeral, she had wrapped a quarter of a tuna sandwich in a napkin to eat later. Justine would be disgusted to see Phoebe at this moment, sitting on a toilet in a public bathroom, eating a spoiling crustless sandwich stolen from a funeral, crying over a line drawing that could have been of anyone, a drawing that had been tossed off in meaningless, drunken seconds.

Phoebe eats the sandwich in four bites, chewing fast. She shoves the sandwich napkin down between her thighs, releases it into the toilet. She stands up, clutching her purse with one hand, zipping her pants clumsily with the other. The stall door clatters open, then closed then open again against its badly painted metallic wall.

She checks her shoes for spatter marks from when the blond man sloshed beer at her feet. He'd just started a game of pool when she entered the bathroom — he will still be bent over the table, sighting a cue. Probably ready for another beer. Phoebe wouldn't mind a game of pool. She's tired of these petty, self-centred women and their jockeying for status, their silly, vain pretensions. One nudge is all it will take to get Justine herding Connie to the car, awash in shredded tissues. Phoebe tosses her purse over her shoulder, runs her hands under cold water, checks her teeth for tuna before returning to the table.

Bartender art

It started simply enough, when a barfly named Dave showed me a photo on his cell phone — a horse he'd built from twigs he found in city parks. He strung the twigs together roughly with loops of barbed wire, and it was oddly beautiful. My bosses, Chip and Max, think he did it to impress me, and that may be partly true, but I've known plenty of artists, and they really can't keep still until they've figured out what they need to do to add meaning to their lives. Me, I add booze to their lives. And, apparently, I organize bizarre art exhibits that half the city shows up for, despite being a bartender with zero artistic abilities of my own. Because that's where we are now — the opening night of said art exhibit, and I'm responsible, and people keep touching me, keep thinking we're friends. These touches and connections are not part of my new life: my body is thrilled but shocked. That's what I get for thinking out loud in front of a librarian — those people get shit done.

Leona slides her arm through mine.

"You people get shit done," I say. I resist pulling my arm away.

"It's almost time to open the doors," she says. "We need wine."

Library staff who have the appropriate alcohol-pouring paperwork have been seconded to run the bar, and one of them twists the cap from a bottle of Pinot Noir, pours us each a small plastic glass of wine. Leona and I clink.

"I miss corkscrews," I say. "That was the only badge I got in Brownies."

"And what's with these tiny glasses? They only hold three ounces."

We sink them, hold them out for refills, and exhale deep breaths together as we inspect the room. I've spent the past six weeks running around the city, interviewing bartenders and examining the art they'd bought from customers. Spending more time with Leona than I've spent with any human in nearly a year: at the library, The Walnut Room, where I work, and in coffee shops. Learning to write an exhibition statement. Cheese cubed or sliced? Frames or no frames? Social media?

Everyone knows bartenders act as surrogate parents, marriage counsellors, and life coaches to their clients, but it's a lesser-known fact that we're also early encouragers of their artistic dreams. I've bought pieces because I liked them, or because payday was a week away for some kid who wanted beers with his buddies, or because some woman needed encouragement. Maybe that's what drew me to work at The Walnut Room: Chip and Max cover the walls with work by local artists that gets swapped out every few months — including Chip's curly landscapes — everything on the walls for sale.

Leona and I spent hours preparing for tonight, collecting these amateur pieces of varying quality, most of which wouldn't have otherwise made it into an art show; we matted and framed paintings and drawings in the simple black frames supplied by the library, hung them on the walls, arranged more on easels, grouped the sculptures and ceramics on plinths. The art is lit from above, interspersed with red pot lights that cast strategic glows and shadows against the brown brick walls. Blues music wanders through hidden speakers.

My contributions to the exhibit follow more conservative themes than some of the other bartenders'. Soft ink drawings of wildlife — a rabbit, a gopher, and a coyote. Pencil drawings of swing sets and sand boxes. A tiny watercolour of columbines I'd forgotten about until I pulled it from my dusty storage closet. And the outlier — a fantastically bold blue mermaid, bought only two months before I fled my former city and arrived here. But there's so much more on these walls and plinths, from bartenders across the city, all proving my original premise that bartenders are first responders when it comes to art.

People start to trickle, then pour, through the double gallery doors, and Leona squeezes my arm. "I think you have the answer to your never-ending question," she says. "No, Emily, it's not going to suck."

The library's media machine has come through. My quirky little endeavour turns out to have fascinating sociological implications that will surely be plumbed by academics, journalists, artists, and suburban SUV drivers eager to assert their grasp of trend. The room is noisier than The Walnut Room on a Friday night. People are everywhere, moving from piece to piece, vying to be the first to view these odd offerings by those in search of encouragement and booze money.

"I lost count at ninety people," Leona hisses. "Three city councillors, including Demeter." Demeter is our less than affectionate name for the city councillor who tried to wage a social media war over an exhibit of nudes at the museum a few months ago. We've never forgiven her for using the 'think of the children' hashtag unironically.

One of my bar regulars, Nick, approaches, wine swaying as he gestures toward the walls. "Is it true, Emily? Do you really exchange beer for art?"

I shrug. "Sometimes I give them smokes instead."

Nick's a professor at the university; in The Walnut Room, he drinks cheap scotch and flirts with me, but he also has a PhD and writes abstruse articles that he often can't resist explaining to whoever's close. Tonight, surrounded by all this social commentary just begging to be dissected, he's torn between personas.

"How often does something like this happen — you buying someone's art in the bar?"

"Oh, Nick," I say, "you must know it's a time-honoured tradition."

"Indeed. Van Gogh —"

"But I draw the line at doodle-art."

"Ha, yes. Actually, Van Gogh —"

"Did you know Van Gogh sold some of his most famous paintings for a bowl of stew and an extra bread roll?"

"Yes, of course, the —"

"Picasso did, too. Did you know that?"

Leona yanks me away. "You're an asshole."

"I'm not getting paid to smile and nod right now," I say. "This is *my* party. It's time for the people to humour me for a change, while I pontificate."

Until we started planning this event, I had no idea how much Leona likes to touch people — we usually had the bar between us. Now, I'm almost used to the feel of her warm hand on my arm. I take another drink of my wine and wave at Dave and his barfly buddy, Pete. Dave clutches his tiny plastic glass and shifts from foot to foot. Pete grins like the father of the bride, striking up conversations with everyone who stops to look at Dave's horse. We move from group to group: bartenders I've worked with over the past few months, artists lurking near their work, like Dave, with bemused expressions.

Leona hugs Dave; I stick to a wide smile. His horse really is a fantastic piece — gnarled branches strung together with loops of barbed wire. The effect is weird and skeletal, abstract yet full of life. He left dried leaves on a few of the branches, and they seem to shiver, mane and tail.

"The beautiful piece that started it all," I say, running my fingers over the horse's spine. "I look forward to seeing what you do next." Dave beams, like I've given him flowers, or a free pitcher of draught beer.

I steer Leona toward Demeter, who is appropriate as always in a blue two-piece suit with demurely draped scarf and gold butterfly pin. She's staring at my blue mermaid, at her pendulous breasts. Both her expression, and the mermaid's, are inscrutable, although Demeter's eyes aren't crooked.

I pitch my voice toward the councillor's shoulder. "What I find so fascinating about these pieces is the implication that it's possible to be an unemployed alcoholic and still make a meaningful and beautiful contribution to society."

Leona chokes on her laughter, and a man and a woman enter. He's tall and dark. She's wearing a long green cape with the hood up, her dark hair spilling out the edges. She pushes back the hood, shakes out her hair. Do I imagine the entire room pauses for a moment at the drama of their entrance, or is it just me?

He's gorgeous, but my eyes pull back to her. I've seen versions of this woman a thousand times, sitting at the bar, legs elegantly crossed and sliding out of her long slim skirt. She doesn't stay long, usually one glass of wine. She mingles by asking servers in a disinterested tone if they're working their way through university. Flexes a polite eyebrow if they say no, if they admit they aren't working to improve their station in life.

A group of university types descend and surround her, exclaiming, "Isabel, what do you think of this bartender art concept?"

The caped Isabel studies the drawing before her as I edge away; the dark-eyed man she came with is watching me watch her. I fall in behind two elderly ladies; they stop at a nude torso in charcoal, and I listen, pretending fascination with a coloured pencil sketch of fall leaves skittering across snow.

"Why on earth wouldn't the artist give her arms or legs?"

"You know, Martha, hands and feet are the hardest to draw."

I turn away, smiling, and the dark-eyed man is next to me, his lashes as thick as if he's wearing mascara. My breath catches as our eyes meet, then I'm past him again. My lipstick feels cracked, my nose shiny. My slim black pants and snug grey sweater are inadequate for the occasion.

An arm slides around my waist, and I leap away as if someone just spilled beer on my shoes. It's my boss, Chip.

"Sorry, sweetheart, I forgot your touch phobia." He squeezes me and removes his arm. "This is fabulous. Some of it's hilarious."

"What are you doing here? You're supposed to be working."

"I told Max I was sneaking out for an hour, cruising. What better place to poach staff than in a room full of art-loving bartenders?"

I point to a woman across the room. "Jenna handled an entire room on her own and still made time to talk to me about the art she's bought. Her bar is ugly, and her boss is an asshole. A prime target."

"Thanks for the tip."

"I'm glad you came," I say. "Once you've stolen a bartender, pick out the art you think I bought. We'll see how well you know me."

Glen and Samantha approach. He's a landscape artist — mostly delicate, blurred watercolours filled with hints of movement. She's an interior designer addicted to luxurious colours and fabrics. Regulars at The Walnut Room.

"Look at this crowd," Sam says. "You must be thrilled."

I shrug. "One day I was looking at a twig horse on a cell phone, and the next thing I know we're drinking wine, surrounded by bartender art."

"Yes, this evening is obviously entirely accidental." She squeezes my hand — why am I surrounded by all these touch-happy people? — and heads across the room to congratulate Dave.

"Quick," I say to Glen, "Give me some fancy artist phrases. My 'interesting juxtapositions of light and shadow' line is getting old. I'm about to resort to 'Would you like a twist of lime with that?'"

Glen throws back his head and gives one of those sincere, booming laughs worthy of a Shakespearean actor. And the dark man is beside me again. Fuck, he's beautiful. The wall behind us holds a pencil drawing of a fox — a bad Bateman rip-off. Beside it, a dragon consumes a maiden who screams blankly. The dragon has a lascivious leer as his tongue wraps around the Barbie doll waist of the maiden. Her flowing hair flows, and her billowy dress billows, and her spilly breasts spill from her bodice.

As the men greet each other, I walk to the bar, grab an open bottle of Beaujolais, and return. Isabel is on the other side of the room, waving a languid hand at a Group of Seven-ish painting of orange and grey trees. I fill Glen's glass and mine and look at the man. He nods, and I top up his glass.

Glen says, "Paul's a painter, too."

"I could tell," I gesture at the faint speckles in his hair. "That, or you're going prematurely green."

His eyes are a witchy hazel with dark rings around the iris. When he smiles, his teeth are ridiculously straight and white. "When it's not going well, I run my hands through my hair."

Glen asks him why it's not going well. Paul shrugs. "I don't want to bore anyone." He looks me over — he studies me until I twitch a little — asks if I'm an artist, too.

I shake my head, wave the wine bottle vaguely and walk away as he and Glen begin to talk about why whatever it is he's working on isn't going well. I used to talk to people about their art, but that was another life in another city. I'm out of practice. Here, the most anyone needs from me — the most I offer — is another drink, to laugh at their jokes now and then. Besides, I can't be responsible for staining those dream teeth with tannins.

Leona meets me halfway across the room. "There are over a hundred and sixty people here now. And John wants a photo."

John interviewed us about the exhibit for the *Journal* two weeks ago; we greet him like an old friend.

"Shoot us against the blue mermaid," Leona says. "She matches my eyes."

"I'm partial to the drunken dragon," I say. "He has that devil-may-care look while he chews up the virgin, that real joy in a job well done. Reminds me of my first boyfriend."

John has us take the two pictures from the walls and prop them against our legs. He poses us leaning forward, arms on the tops of the frames. My hair is falling over my shoulders; Leona and I are laughing at the camera and at each other. As my glance skims the room, I see the dark-eyed man — Paul — watching me, unsmiling and intent. My smile fades. The flash goes off.

I abandon colour and noise every day when I leave the cocoon of The Walnut Room. Last night, after the exhibit, I paced my tiny apartment; I could feel movement, just out of sight, barely ahead of me as I drifted from room to room. Shifts of light and dark from the corner of my eye, nothing there when I turned my head to try to catch it full on. Something brushed past my right leg, and I looked down, my hand instinctively reaching out at knee height.

"Where are you?" I said. "Please." My open fingers caressing nothing but air. Eventually, I went to bed.

And this morning, I sit on the couch for so long, legs curled under me, that I stagger when I eventually stand. I flex my legs, clear my throat, prepare for contact. In the daylight, the air doesn't move as oddly: dust motes linger undisturbed in the space between window and couch. The living room floor is scattered with remnants of the Bartender Art exhibit — pieces that didn't make the cut, other paper detritus from my former life that got mixed in with the boxes labelled 'art.' I step over them and dump my cold coffee in the sink. I refill my mug, hold its warmth against my chest, settle back into the couch.

A small painting of a green dog, its orange tongue lolling, sits on my coffee table: my heart thuds up against my rib cage, and I blink fast to clear my vision. I couldn't bear to put it in the show, but some perverse piece of me refused to hide it away again. My gaze skips past it to the window, and I watch the world past this tiny wooden rectangle — a flock of birds that sweeps and tumbles through the air in a hypnotic pattern — a murmuration, I think it's called. They dive in and out of frame, and I stare at the patch of sky, wait to see if they'll return.

The hours leak away. I walk to the bathroom, pull a few curls from the clip holding back my hair, let them fall around my face. I apply a second coat of mascara. I don't speak until I walk in the door of The Walnut Room at four o'clock.

Glen and Samantha sit at the bar, reading the story the *Journal* ran about opening night. Sam smooths out the lines and turns it toward me like an offering. Leona and me, leaning on our chosen pictures.

Leona is laughing, her long, elegant hands draped over the frame of the blue mermaid. My fingers are curled, nails sliding against the picture frame, as if I'm about to reach for something.

"Why do you look so serious?" Sam asks. "You were having the time of your life."

I shrug. "Post-party let-down, maybe."

"I hear you've turned down a few offers for the blue mermaid," Glen says.

Max comes out from the back, wiping his hands on a towel. "I made an offer on that mermaid. Chip nearly choked on his cannoli."

"I couldn't part with her after finally getting public permission to love her," I say. "But I was surprised how many offers were made on the paintings, and how many bartenders turned them down. Tacky is the new cool, apparently."

"Dave says he's got three commissions for horses," Sam says.

"Yes, the whole show grew unexpected legs," I say. "It's so —"

Max laughs. "Why do you sound surprised? You invited this in."

The bar fills up. The after-work crowd morphs into the supper crowd. Laughter and words rise like bubbles over the jazz radio station. Beer, wine, designer martinis for what looks like a

Mary Kay mini-convention. Chip and Max are back and forth to the kitchen, delivering fragrant bowls of Thai soup, cannelloni, and shepherd's pie. We fall into our dance, moving fast, side by side, reaching around each other for bottles, glasses, slices of lemon.

Every time the wooden door opens and closes, I lift my head, and my breath catches for a second, releasing again at the sight of another regular. In between delivering drinks, I smooth my clothes, sneak glances in the bar mirrors. The dim lights, the cinnamon walls, and the hanging art cast flickering echoes of the exhibit, the magical momentary space we'd created in the library auditorium. The sense of promise lingers, but it's fading.

I follow Chip to the kitchen and arrange black and green olives around the perimeter of yellow serving dishes while he heaps hummus in their centres. The smell of garlic fills the room.

"How do people do it?"

"Do what?"

"Create. How do you know you can?"

"You just do it," Chip says. "You take a class, you play. You keep trying until you make something you like. Or at least that you don't hate completely."

"I don't make anything," I say.

"You should come over Sunday," Chip says. "Max will cook dinner. We'll drink wine and solve all the problems of the world."

We both know I'm not going to accept. I never do. I go back out front to check on my customers.

A thin man by the window with carefully combed hair gestures that he needs another scotch. He stares into his drink for two hours every Saturday. He doesn't talk much, to me or to the other regulars. He doesn't tip much, either, but I don't take it personally. If I didn't work in a bar, I'd probably have a similar ritual, if only to keep my voice from rusting.

I serve drinks all night, reject an offer from a suit and tie to go for a drink next week; I'm not as gracious as usual in my barfly rejection. His tie was red and blue, diagonal stripes, his smile blurred and loose. I go home at two a.m., my restless stomach protesting in dismay. Is this it? Can this be it?

It takes Paul a week to show up at The Walnut Room. A week in which I smile and pour drinks while everyone else gets on with their big adventures. Dave is experimenting with variations; he has a commission for a tree branch skunk. Pete's been inspired, too: he's a welder, and now he's playing at welding metal sculptures in his garage. The two of them flank Leona at the bar, showing her photos on their cell phones.

"It's ugly and lumpy, but I'm having a hell of a time," Pete says to Leona. "Once I get good enough, I'll make something for you."

"I like ugly, lumpy art," she says. "Sometimes I write ugly, lumpy poetry."

Pete's pieces are clumsy but intriguing; rougher versions of a fish sculpture I didn't buy, years ago, in Cuba — bits of scrap metal, screws, and twisted silverware layered over each other to create a surprisingly delicate piece I've never forgotten.

The door swings open; six young women pour in — hair stylists, I'm guessing, from the freshly glistening heads of magenta, orange, platinum blonde, and deep black. Cranberry vodka shots all around, followed by a piña colada, two White Russians, two vodka paralyzers, and a tequila sunrise, lots of cherries and orange slices.

They shoot back the cranberry vodka, confirm my hair is naturally curly, and replace the glasses on my tray. The door sounds behind me, and the hairdresser with glossy black hair says, "Ooh, a little old for me, but very cute."

Paul is looking around the room, surveying, before his gaze comes to rest on me. I walk to the bar to put down my tray. He chooses a table at the back. I pour Leona, Dave, and Pete another round without asking; then I take a deep breath, and I go.

He's wearing faded jeans and a soft denim shirt, sleeves rolled up to the elbows. White T-shirt underneath. The dark hairs on his arms trail to bony wrists and large, knobby hands. His fingers are flecked with paint.

"Hello, Emily." His eyes are all over my face, my hair. "Nice place."

"I bought all the art myself," I say. I want to say, "What the fuck took you so long?" But when he orders a dark ale and a glass of white wine, I'm glad I didn't.

I confirm whether his date wants the house wine or a Sauvignon Blanc, turn back to the bar. My shirt lifts as I reach to the hanging rack above the bar for a pint glass, exposes an inch of midriff. My breath is uneven as I pull the dark, foaming ale. This, this is what I've been pacing around all week for? And he's bringing his date? I slosh the wine, ostentatiously pull a fresh cloth from beneath the bar to wipe the thin drizzle from the side of her glass.

Max is sprinkling pink sea salt on a heap of roasted cauliflower in a blue bowl. "Everything okay?"

"Fine, thanks." I take the beer and wine back to the table, set the beer in front of Paul, the wine at the chair next to his. "If you're interested in food, Max has several creations simmering tonight."

His eyes don't leave me as the door opens again behind us, as he shakes his head.

"Isn't she glamorous," the magenta hairdresser whispers.

I throw a general smile in the direction of the door. "That's everything, then?" I beat it back to the bar as Isabel settles beside Paul. She arranges her cape loosely around her shoulders, flicks her disinterested gaze across the room before turning to him.

"Nice," Max says as I slide behind him at the bar. He hands me an anchovy-stuffed green olive.

"The woman in green?"

"It was nice of her to leave the windy moors to grace us with her presence," he says. "But no, I meant the guy with her."

"Stick with Chip. That one looks like a heartbreaker." I bite into the olive. Max raises his eyebrows. I fiddle with the tub of garnishes, wipe the counter until he disappears into the kitchen again.

Leona jerks her head discreetly toward the back table. "Weren't they at the opening?"

I nod. She mouths "gorgeous" and picks up her wine. I cross my eyes so only she can see it, am pleased when she chokes on her Pinot noir.

The noise level rises as the bar fills up. Max and I move from table to table with platters of ribs, bowls of Thai soup, chili with homemade corn bread. Drinks and more drinks. Every time I look to see if Paul and Isabel need more drinks, they are deep in conversation. She leans forward as she talks; he sprawls back in his chair.

And then he approaches the bar. "She's on the phone. I was getting restless, thought I'd say hello." He hoists his glass at me and drinks.

I hate him, and my nipples are hard. Why is he here with her? I move down the bar, away from Dave, Pete, and Leona. Max is pulling glasses out of the dishwasher, his studied indifference to us palpable.

Paul picks up one of the burnished metal coasters, flipping it in his long fingers. "It's nice to see you again."

"Why are you here?"

"Glen said it was a great place." He is looking me up and down. It's not lascivious, just thorough and keen. I start to cross my arms over my breasts, relax them again at my sides.

Let him look. I raise an eyebrow and wait.

"I've been thinking about you," he says.

"How so?"

"What you did with the exhibit. Why you did it. I was watching you."

Someone calls my name. I ignore it, and Max moves toward them. Paul relaxes against the bar, sips his beer. "I have some business to take care of right now. But I'd like to see you."

The hairdressers are calling for another round of shots. "Excuse me," I say. "My fans await."

He watches as I pour cranberry vodka into six shot glasses and place them on a tray. I pause in front of him. At the back of the room, Isabel sets her phone and purse on the table and stands, slides her stupid cape around her shoulders. His breath stirs the curls at my temples. "You know where to find me," I say. I walk past him and don't look up as the door swings shut behind them.

The rest of the night is a blur of movement, noise, and clinking glasses. When the last customers have left, I scrub at the bar until Max takes the cloth from my hand. "Emily, sit down. We're done."

He pours us each a big glass of cabernet. "That man left you a big tip. Huge, actually."

"I don't want to know." I slump against the bar, adrenalin crashing out of me in waves.

Max pulls a cigarette out of his breast pocket, waves it.

"Fuck, yes," I say. It's our occasional secret. We walk out the back door, sit on the steps next to the blue dumpster. Max lights it and passes it to me. My shoulders and chest expand to draw the familiar smoke deep inside me. I lean my head against his warm shoulder, and he looks at me, surprised. The tip of the cigarette sparks bright, then dull red; we inhale and release, passing it back and forth. The tendrils of smoke twine and shimmer around our heads and dissipate into the night.

As I walk into my dark bedroom, I feel a swish of movement behind me, a shift in the air that makes the skin on my ankles tingle. I freeze, but it wisps away again; the only sounds in the empty room are my bare feet padding against the thin carpet, the click of the switch at the base of the bedside lamp.

I lie awake for hours, wake early to balance it out; my head pounds as though Max and I had finished all the wine in The Walnut Room, all the wine in the world.

I prop open the window and curl up on the couch; road dust and sand from the winter streets float in on the morning air, overtaken by the soft flirtations of spring, its hints of budding greens. I've cleaned up most of the detritus that was spread across the floor, stowed it safely back in the storage room among all the taped-up boxes from my former life. The place looks barely lived in — the walls are bare, the furniture sparse. There's one low bookshelf against a wall, and the table surfaces are empty other than lamps, the remote controls. When I moved here, I gave my plants away or threw them in the garbage. No living being other than me has set foot in the place since the day my landlord handed over the keys.

The green dog with the orange tongue grins at me from the table; my gaze skips past, refusing to rest there, to take in any detail.

The bar is quiet when I arrive, the lure of sunshine stronger than the lure of day drinking. I pace around, wash tables, and check the lime stocks.

Chip examines my face. "I like this look. Kind of dissipated. The black bags under your eyes bring out the blue."

I groan. "Can we put up a sign today? Management requests that all tips be nice, quiet bills rather than noisy, clinking coins."

He massages my shoulders, and I let myself lean back against his broad chest. Max is in and out of the kitchen, working on the supper specials. The comforting smell of garlic permeates the room.

Two women at the back are deep in conversation about teenagers. They don't need anything. A man at one of the small, high tables needs a beer. The couple in the corner drag their eyes from each other long enough to order two more martinis. I drop off the drinks, pour myself another coffee. It's going to be a long shift.

That's when the wooden door swings open, and Paul enters.

Max says, "And the moment we've all been waiting for has arrived."

"I know," I say. "Big trouble for moose and squirrel."

"I want you to pose for me," Paul says, lifting a lock of curls from my shoulder. He said it first in the bar; he walked straight toward me. I met him before he was halfway across the room, and he said it without preamble, while we were still in motion toward each other.

The bar had shrunk to three shimmering inches between us — to the chest I was about to put my hand on — when Chip nudged me with his elbow. He walked past us to set a bloody Mary and a lager on the table in the corner booth, said the bar was too quiet, I should take the afternoon off. Paul and I sank into the booth and lifted our drinks to our mouths. I put my finger on his freckled forearm, ran it up and down the tendon in his wrist. He turned his hand and closed it over my finger. I was barely breathing. Did we talk? We must have said words. When our drinks were half empty, we stood and left The Walnut Room. His hand was large and firm between my legs as we drove to his house, tapping at me lightly with two long fingers. Large sun-filled rooms with low bookshelves lined high white walls, and before the door had closed, we were pulling at each other's clothes, he was pushing me up against the entryway wall. He took my hand, and I stumbled with him up the stairs. I came before he pushed inside me, then again when he did.

Now, he says it again: "I want you to pose for me." He twines my hair around his finger, his hand brushing my collarbone. He slides his finger from the ringlet, pulls it straight, watches it bounce back.

I'm lying across his chest, watching his eyes as he plays with my hair. We're half under a yellow comforter, rust and amber cushions kicked to the floor. The bed is plushy and soft; the walls are white and bare. The dresser holds a stack of books, carelessly piled. A watch. A sheaf of papers. Sunlight dapples through the blinds, layering his face in greens and yellows. His chest gleams with a light film of sweat; I lean forward to lick it. His salt on my tongue.

"Why do you want me to pose?" Will he say it's because I'm beautiful?

"When I saw you at the exhibit, I knew I wanted those eyes. This hair." He tangles his fingers in my mess of curls, tugs. "And that little smile you gave when you were eavesdropping on the old ladies." He runs his finger over the corner of my mouth.

I am still, afraid to break this fragile moment, to have him see only my regular face with its flaws.

He pulls my hair around my shoulders, arranges it over my breasts. Every inch of my skin, every strand of my hair, arches under his touch like a cat.

"Tell me," I whisper, "What you want me for."

He slides from under me, walks naked from the room, returns with two books. He settles against the headboard, and I pull the sheet up between my legs to loosely cover my breasts. He opens the books, flipping quickly to the photographs he wants — marble statues of women: The Korai. Their hair. Their smiles.

One in particular catches my attention. Antenor's Kore is breathtaking: her nose is missing, and the gash extends to her forehead. Her eyes are darker than the other statues; they are rock crystal, set in lead. She's draped in flowing fabric. Her hair falls to just above her breasts — four perfect, crimped ringlets on each side. Her fingers are missing on the hand hanging at her side, and the right arm is broken off where it would extend from her sleeve.

Another, the Peplos Kore, has eyes more typical of the Greek statues I've seen, slightly protruding marble, blank and vaguely blind, with only hints of the original bright paint still clinging to crevices in the aged stone. Her hair falls in three long ringlets over each shoulder, framing but not covering her stone breasts. Her drapery hangs straight and slim against her legs. She, too, is missing the arm that would extend toward the viewer. The tips of her breasts are chipped away.

Both statues smile slightly, lips barely turned up as they stare out from the page.

"They look like the Mona Lisa."

"The archaic smile," he says. "It was a convention of the time, but you can see some differences in the smiles when you start looking."

"This is what I remind you of? Women with broken hands and Stepford Wife mouths?"

They are similar in pose and expression, but he's right, the nuances within the archaic smile are vast. They are all damaged in various ways, and magnificent, Amazons about to stride from the page, broad shouldered and slim hipped. Those who still have arms hold out offerings to Athena: pomegranates, birds, chunks of marble no longer recognizable as the gifts they were intended to be.

The bed shifts, and Paul offers me a glass of wine.

"What do you want from me?" I ask. "How does this connect to me?"

He shakes his head. "I can't describe it. I need you to pose for me."

I nod. I drink, breathing in the dark red on my tongue, aware of my hair straggling over my naked breasts, of my rising excitement.

At work, I pour beer and make jokes, and all I can think of is skin, his and mine. Greek sculpture, my hair, the way he bit my ear lightly, his tapping fingers, how many times I came. My flesh crawls with desire.

At home, I look at myself in the mirror, try on variations of the archaic smile. I touch myself, my lips, my breasts. I shake my hair loose from its clip every night and feel him pulling it, pulling my head back over the edge of the bed as he thrusts into me. I roam my apartment, running my fingers over the bare, white walls. Shadows flicker at the edge of my vision. My finger is in my mouth, my tongue tracing it. The telephone doesn't ring.

At work, three men ask me out. I have to bite my tongue at my impatience with them. Leona invites me to go for a drink. I start to refuse, then I pause, then I accept. She acts as though this is normal.

"Stop giving me that look," I say to Max. "I have no comment."

Leona and I choose a bar near the library, three blocks from everyone we know at The Walnut Room. It's been two weeks since the exhibit. A week since Paul finally appeared. Three days since I followed him home as though he'd buttered my paws. I haven't heard from him since. He'd told me he had things to take care of. Is he still disentangling himself from the Caped Isabel?

Leona studies me as she slides into the booth, squirming out of her apple green jacket. "You look different."

"It's the hair. Some days it just sticks out all over the place."

"Save that shit for the drunks," she says. "You're freshly fucked, and you're freaked out about it."

"Is it that obvious?"

"Only to me. And to Chip and Max."

"You've been talking about me?"

"That's what friends are for," she says. "To talk about you behind your back."

"You're not going to let me avoid this, are you?"

Leona laughs, then she leans forward and takes my hand. "You've avoided a lot of discussions with all of us for a long time, but I'm not letting this pass. We're friends, Em. Put out or get out."

I want to pull my hand away, but I don't. I take a big swallow of wine, then another. I start to talk. The dead marriage — the city and past I fled — is easier to talk about than my dead dog, his unsatisfactory hauntings, and my empty, terrible fear.

Three easels hold paintings in various stages of progress; more sketches for this new series litter the floor. The studio at the back of Paul's house is spacious and filled with sunlight this late afternoon. After being on my feet all day, I'm relieved to sit, that today's focus is on necks and faces. His hands move across the canvas, and I pull the blanket across my lap. Our meetings are a strange mix, every time, of heat and distance, sex and dissociation. I climb him when we meet, I attempt to devour him; in return, he pulls off my clothes and studies my shoulders, my clavicles. I wait each night — patiently or anxiously — for my reward, drifting and floating through my thoughts until the moment he sets aside his brushes and pencils.

"Do you ever worry that I won't like the paintings?"

"The thought hadn't crossed my mind."

"Now that I've brought it up, will you be worried?"

He shakes his head, looks back at the canvas. "Whether you like it or not isn't the point."

Sometimes he tells me about painters he admires, or talks about paint itself, textures and mark-making. His voice will dwindle away in mid-sentence. I sit in silence or tell desultory stories about bar customers or situations that caught my attention. I tell him that Leona joined a writing group and has started submitting poems to journals. I describe photographs I've seen of Pete's welded sculptures. It's as though I'm talking to myself. I don't mind being ignored; there's something comforting about hearing my voice winding through the white room, brushing the bare surfaces without touching down.

He doesn't run his hands through his hair in our sessions. His long hands move rapidly from paint to canvas. I stretch again, wondering how much longer until he cleans his brushes and turns the painting to the wall, dreaming of what those hands will do.

"What are you thinking about?"

"This and that."

"Your face is too soft. I need it blank."

I feel a flash of anger, rejection.

"That's better," he says.

The next week, Chip invites me and Paul over for dinner. The thought of Paul making polite conversation with strangers over a meal startles me. I can't imagine it — us, together, doing something so ordinary. Paul has never even been to my apartment; I don't think he knows where I live.

"We can't," I say. I run a fresh cloth under the hot tap, wring it out. "He's obsessed with the series."

Chip says to Leona, "She always wipes the bar down when she's nervous. Have you noticed that?"

I throw the cloth at him. "I have a lot on my mind. In a month or so, everyone's going to see my naked breasts. It's a lot to process."

Chip's mouth gapes, and he shakes his finger at Leona. "You most definitely did not tell me the naked part."

"Sorry. My loyalties were divided."

"When do we get to see these delicious breasts?" Chip asks. "Lord, Dave's going to have to get a second mortgage so he can buy the entire series."

I wince. "I know nothing. I'm just the muse."

"I'm curious," Leona says, "how being a model for obsession is inspiring your own creativity?"

"I'm not an artist."

Chip and Leona look at each other. "We think you are," Chip says.

"On what basis? And will you two stop talking about me when I'm not here?"

Leona pats Chip's hand. "It's okay. We'll just talk about her to Max, and he can pass messages."

"I'm inspiring a well-known, successful artist," I say. "That can be my contribution to the world."

"Mine's literacy," Leona says. "Oh, and poetry."

"Mine's cannelloni," Chip says. "And painting."

"You can both fuck off."

I can't do what Paul does. He can't even do it himself tonight. First, he had me sitting on a stool, then standing by the window. Arms up, arms out, sheet covering breast, then draped below it while he moved from canvas to canvas stroking quick lines. Now he throws down his charcoal. "Forget it."

His dark eyes look through me, beyond me, for something I'm not giving him. I grab the grey terrycloth robe and pull it tight around me, sit cross-legged on the couch.

"What's the matter with you tonight?" he asks.

"This is my fault?" I push my hair back from my face. "My back is killing me. I've been pouring beer for eight hours, listening to the same sad stories."

"Tell me a sad story," he says.

"Like what? I'm not exactly bursting with ideas."

"Tell me something dark and ugly from your past."

I sift through the past few years, shove those stories away. Paul and I don't talk about exes or grief. The intensity of his gaze irritates me tonight, and I run through options, watching how his focus tightens in on me.

"You want something dark and ugly? How's this? My grandfather groped me when I was fourteen."

He nods, and I settle back on the couch, sink my aching back into the cushions. I take my time starting.

"I was fourteen — no, I was thirteen — when he started staring at me. He kept comparing me to a budding flower."

He makes a sound of disgust; he's all mine now, fascinated. My voice gets harder. "He was sitting in the kitchen one night, talking with my mother while she made supper. He wanted a hug. I gave him an awkward one from the side."

He picks up his pad and charcoal, makes lines on the paper while I talk, his eyes intent on me. He nods again when I pause.

"That wasn't good enough. He said he wanted a 'real hug.' My mother turned from the stove and smiled at us."

He's drawing more quickly, his eyes flick back and forth between the paper and my face.

"So, I leaned in, and he groped my breast. My mother didn't see, or she chose not to see. And I didn't say a word."

"Don't change a thing about your face," he says. His pencil flashes across the page. He tears it off and starts a new one.

I've been leaning forward, my robe gaping. I pull it tight at my neck now, sit back and watch his hand fly across the page in short, bursty strokes. I walk to the window.

"You're beautiful," he says. He puts down his pencil and crosses the room, pulls me to the floor. He slides his hand under the robe and strokes me. When he removes the robe and begins to trace my collarbone, I knock his hand away.

I get up, take a piece of charcoal from the table. I remove his shirt, draw rough eyes on his chest — closed eyes, open eyes, eyes with Xs in place of pupils. I draw snakes on his arms and smear grey lines across his face. I push into his flesh with the pencil, bite his shoulder, taste the bitter charcoal in my mouth. His skin is taut across his clavicle, my hands are blackened; my teeth pinch sharply into his flesh. He winces. I look at his witchy eyes, press in, bite him again. A little harder.

Isabel comes looking for me, her green cape swirling as she selects a table in the centre of the room.

"Emily, isn't it?" Her pale, manicured fingers smooth out the folds of fabric across the back of her chair. "I saw you at your bartender event, of course, and Paul talks about you now and then."

"How kind of him to remember." My heart hammers at my chest, at the back of my throat. "Please, have a seat. Shall I bring you some white wine?"

"Thank you." She sets her bag on a chair, moves to the wall to study the paintings.

I polish her glass with a clean towel as she slithers around the room. Max appears beside me.

"Isn't that . . . ?"

"Fuck, you have a good memory."

He touches my hand, below the bar where she can't see. "Do you want me to look after her?"

I shake my head. "She's here for a reason. I might as well find out what it is." I take a deep breath, pour her wine from a fresh bottle and take it to her table. She returns and sinks against her glowing green backdrop.

"Max has Moroccan lamb bites on tonight if you're interested."

She shakes her head.

"Is there anything else?" I look around the room, wishing it were busier.

"The series is coming along nicely."

"It is, from what I can tell."

"It's good to see Paul working again. He was in a bit of a dry spell until he saw you — your hair." She smiles at me, crosses one long leg over the other. My own smile becomes more genuine; I remember imagining her doing this, with just that studied grace, the first time I set eyes on her.

"My hair has launched ships," I say. "And been used for bungee jumping."

She flicks at her phone to check the time. "Paul will be here shortly. You can bring him the usual."

I check my watch. "I'm off shift, but I'll make sure Max keeps an eye on the door if I miss him."

Max is flashing me Jesus eyes; he isn't surprised when I say, "I know I've only been here an hour, but my shift just ended. I'm sorry."

"No problem," he says. "Jenna will be here in an hour." He gestures toward Isabel. "Should I accidentally spill a drink on your friend?"

"She'd melt, and what a mess you'd have to clean up," I say. "But you would get a nice pair of ruby slippers." Max follows me into the back. "I love you for not asking questions," I say. My hands are shaking. "Her date will want a pint of dark ale. He'll be here any minute."

Max rummages in the back of a drawer, hands me a cigarette and a book of matches. I kiss his cheek, escape out the back door.

I follow wooden steps into the river valley, walking fast, trying to stop shaking. I can't believe I've opened myself to this again. And I can't believe the instrument of my torture is some bitch in a melodramatic cape, of all the ridiculous things. I stop, finally, and sit on a bench, light the cigarette. A jogger puffs toward me, glares at the trail of smoke coming from my hand. I exhale after her in a solid, vicious stream. "Get a cape," I say. "I can't take you seriously in spandex."

I am stabbed with fierce, primitive hatred — for myself, for her, for him. I hear him saying my name to her, casually, as they have civilized drinks together. Before what? Before stripping off their clothes and fucking? My mind is jammed with images of the two of us, the two of them. He thrusting into her, pulling at her hair the way he's done with me. What I thought was an awakening, something meaningful, is cheap sex — ugly, humiliating. I was better off living alone in my cave. I stub the cigarette in a patch of dirt, put the butt in my pocket and go home.

I sit on my couch in my naked room, fingernails digging into my palms. I hiss to myself, but my eyes stay dry. I will myself to blankness, but it won't come. The green dog with the orange tongue is smiling at me. Finally, I lean forward, trace my fingers over the upright green ears again and again, over that cockeyed, goofy grin.

Paul calls the next day, the usual summons; exhausted, I respond like one of Pavlov's dogs. I walk into his studio, wait for him to come to me. He runs his hand through his hair as he approaches.

"I need you," he says. He pulls me toward him. "You look tired." His eyes search my face, but not for pain.

I look at his hands, at the rough knuckles, the paint on his fingers. He leads me to the window, removes my shirt and drapes me in soft fabric. He unclips my hair, pulls it carelessly over my shoulders. He stands back to view me, then steps in and bends his head to me, bites the tendon in my neck. I arch into him. At this moment, Isabel means nothing to him. I am all he sees.

Later he tells me she's his agent. This is how little we talk — I'd never asked about their relationship. She's set up a touring exhibit, kicking off with one of the best galleries in the city, followed by fifteen major centres across Canada, massive arts funding.

"Congratulations," I say. "Are you fucking her?"

"Not right now."

He has. He will again. He has stripped me and painted me, and we are near the end, I think. But I started something with my bartender art, and it's not going to end with me hanging on a wall. I run my hand over his flat stomach, breathe in paint and sweat. Almost finished, but not quite. I open myself to him, wider than ever, and he floods me — I am bruised, raw, and somehow inspired.

I stopped looking at the paintings before they were completed; he was distracted, pacing from easels to sketches to me, and back. He didn't need me for the final two weeks; I didn't see or hear from him. I poured drinks and looked out windows and walked the trails in the river valley, studying fallen branches, absently pocketing small pieces of metal discarded or lost at the edges of the paths.

I took the green dog and the blue mermaid to an art store; I had them framed. I used a level. I measured. I made light pencil marks on the wall. Then I took a breath, and I swung the hammer, tapping into the walls. They hang opposite my couch: I'm practising being able to look from mermaid breasts to dog.

And now here we are, Leona and me, wine in hand, at Paul's opening night. The gallery is full of artists, patrons, my friends.

Isabel floats through the room greeting people, somehow smaller without her cape, which she has reluctantly abandoned now that it's late summer and the nights are warm and bright. Paul stands in the centre of the room, smiling politely at the people clustered around him. It's the same expression he wore when, early on, I asked where he grew up, whether he'd painted in high school.

"My god," Leona breathes. "I hope Demeter shows up to see these."

"Me too," I say. "We're overdue for a scandal in this town."

The twelve paintings incorporate the classic poses of Greek Korai, but the women — me — are dressed, or partially dressed, in contemporary clothing, with vague blurs of contemporary settings behind them. Many have stumps instead of arms, or bleeding gashes in their foreheads. Their mouths curve in variations of the archaic smile; their eyes reflect horror, exhaustion, sorrow. They are pale, like washed marble, their red lips and dark eyes the only colour on their faces. Their hair curls into geometrical ringlets that outline their breasts.

"What do you think?"

"They're horrifying and mesmerizing. Very skillful. How do you feel about being painted like this?"

"It's not me," I say. "He was never really looking at me while he was painting."

Leona studies my face.

"Cut the compassion crap," I tell her. "We're being light and witty tonight." I jerk my head toward Dave and Pete, who are muttering to each other, shaking their heads. "I'm having an easier time viewing them objectively than the guys are."

Leona glances at them, laughs. "If they're having trouble with this, I better not let them read some of the dark sex poems I've been working on."

"Ah, dark sex," I say. "I'm going to miss that."

We look at Paul, his shirtsleeves rolled to the elbows, white T-shirt underneath, faded jeans. His hair falls across his forehead. "Was it as incredible as I think?"

A sharp pang hits my chest, clutches at my breath, then releases. "Fuck, yes."

I squeeze between Chip and Max, who are studying a painting of a woman with blank eyes; she's balancing a martini glass with two olives on a spear, above her head, on the bleeding stump of her arm.

"I promise not to do that at the bar," I say.

"I hate them," Max says.

"I sort of love them," Chip says.

"I love you both," I say, hugging them.

I stand in front of the painting Paul did after I told him those lies about my poor, maligned grandfather. The woman's face is lost and angry, her eyes dark as rock crystal set in lead. She wears a ripped garment that exposes the slash of red skin where her left breast should be. She holds a bloody stuffed bear in her outstretched hand.

I feel him behind me. "I've heard a few people wondering if you hate women," I say.

His fingers brush my neck, tug on a ringlet. "On the contrary."

My skin tingles. "I'm trying to understand what goes through an artist's mind in order to create images like this."

He frowns and I laugh. "Don't worry." I touch his forearm. "I'm not asking you. I'll find out on my own. I prefer to remember you as my demon lover."

His eyes flash with amusement. His fingers slide to the inside of my wrist, stroke my pulse point.

"Excuse me." I pull my hand away. "I have to talk to a friend."

Isabel stands at the bar. As I cross the room, strangers steal looks at me, the woman in the paintings. I'd spent considerable time deciding whether I should put my hair up, but eventually opted for the usual curls, pinned at the top of my head and cascading over my shoulders. I'm wearing all black, a long slim dress with a high slit that flashes leg as I move. The background music has a steady, silvery beat and I match my pace to it as I approach her.

"I wanted to congratulate you," I say. "I see stickers on two of the paintings."

"He's so talented," she says, looking me up and down.

I have briefly won this little struggle with Isabel; after all, the walls are hung with images of me, not her. The irony is that we both thought that was the struggle we should be focusing on. That being painted by someone else — being hung on their wall — was the prize.

Paul is watching us from across the room.

"That he is," I say. I raise my glass to him and then tip it to her. "Good luck, Isabel."

And I mean it. My invisible cape swishes around my legs as I stride to the door. Leona is waiting for me; we're on our way to meet our friends at The Walnut Room. And next week, I think I'll learn to weld.

Children in the walls

I was too aware of the faint squelching sound my shoes were
making to notice that the husband and wife were hissing at each
other in the pantry; Tony jerked his head toward the etched glass
doors to alert me. It had rained earlier, and I hadn't been able to
avoid the puddles collected in the driveway as I carried tub after
tub of food, glassware, and utensils from the van into the house.
Now, the husband kicked the door shut on their argument. I
lowered my eyes even as his slid over me, unseeing.

It was the sort of house you saw on television, not a regular
house where people take their shoes off. I willed away all thought
of shoe noises and counted on the cloak of invisibility that
had surrounded me for most of my life. Tony slid trays of beef
tenderloin into a stacked double oven while I set up the bar.

The kitchen was larger than my apartment, bright and
modern, in contrast to my first impression of the house. As we
had driven up the winding driveway, heavy-bottomed clouds
were gathering, pushing away the pale blue that had edged in
after the morning's steady drizzle. The house loomed alone at the
top of a hill, the treetops fingering the sills of its second-story
windows. Its grey stone façade blended into the blackening sky
behind it, and the lights that glowed from every window seemed
to beckon warmth and refuge.

The husband's smile and handshake were big when he
first greeted us, everything about him slightly oversized as he
directed us around the kitchen. He wasn't smiling now, as he
and his wife emerged from the pantry. He looked like a rich man

— large and confident in a deep purple button-down shirt with the sleeves rolled to his forearms. My thin goatee felt wispy and insubstantial, and I wondered about shaving it the next morning.

The wife was too thin, in high heels and a little black dress that exposed most of her back. Her hair was straight, deep chocolate brown, almost to her waist. She flashed Tony a bright social face; her husband's impatience smoothed out as he viewed our array of glassware, utensils, and food.

"Do you boys need anything?" He directed his question to Tony, who flicked his eyes sideways but otherwise kept himself from bristling at being lumped in with the likes of me: a gangly student with bad facial hair. He assured the husband all was on schedule. Our host nodded and walked away.

The wife peered into the tubs of food and exclaimed over the menu. She shook her head in ways that didn't match her words, but set her hair stroking and gliding over the bare skin of her shoulders and back. I kept my eyes down as I unpacked. Tony had warned me early on to keep my eyes away from the women we served. He didn't follow his own advice, but I didn't argue. I had enough difficulty talking to Lindsay, the girl I'd been trying to get close to all semester. Rich women were laughably out of my reach.

I removed flutes and goblets from boxes and polished them with a soft cloth. The hosts owned more glassware than Tony's well-stocked catering kitchen, but it was part of the service — our delivery of everything that was needed, and then our removal of it again — feasts laid before the king and queen like magic, all evidence whisked away afterward. We tiptoed backwards out of their lives, brushing over our footsteps to erase every sign of our presence.

The wife wouldn't touch most of the food, I was certain. I'd been working for Tony for a year, earning university tuition, catering private parties. The women fell into two categories: those who pretended to love food but didn't eat, and those who ate everything in sight. Rich men didn't have a problem with food or drink. They strode through parties like kings, consuming what they craved, walking away from what they didn't.

Tony gestured to the trays of melon wrapped in prosciutto, describing how baking them would meld the salty and sweet flavours. His voice deepened and his shaggy blonde head leaned in closer to the wife's as he spoke. "It's a flavour explosion in your mouth."

"You make it sound so naughty."

Their laughter sounded delinquent. If I spoke that way to Lindsay she'd laugh, and I'd be rendered less visible than ever. Lindsay, however, would eat the food rather than merely talking about it.

A little girl ran down the stairs. "When are they coming?"

"Soon." The woman held the girl at arm's length, looked her up and down. "Change into a dance costume, Felicia. You want to create an impression." The girl nodded and ran back upstairs. I watched her go, unsure why the sight of her was unsettling. Her long, dark hair bounced on her back as she retreated, and I realized, then, she had the hair of an adult. At six or seven, which is how old I estimated this child to be, her hair was thick and abundant, springing from her scalp aggressively, more like a wig than human hair. Oddly dark, as if it had been coloured.

Guests began to arrive, some with wispy-haired children who disappeared upstairs. The wife slid through the room, hugging everyone. Her hands moved emphatically, like the drama students at school who were never not performing: acutely aware of the people going by, of how they were seen.

I poured drinks under the husband's supervision. The room filled, and the noise increased. The wife had her hand on her husband's arm, the perfect couple. Women admired the décor. Men admired the scotch.

The little girl ran through the kitchen with a boy behind her. The boy knocked against Tony as he removed trays from the oven. Tony kneed the oven door closed and smiled down as though he liked children. I arranged the prosciutto melon bites on large platters as the wife pulled the girl to her.

"Felicia, you're a dancer. Move like one." She bent to look into the child's eyes; they were nose to nose. "Body awareness," she said. "Remember?"

The husband stepped up then and tousled the girl's thick hair. "Go play with your friends. We'll bring supper up soon."

Felicia continued to stare into her mother's eyes. They were a silent bubble in the centre of the noisy room, and I strained to hear. "Don't eat too much," the mother said. "And nothing messy. You have to dance."

Felicia smiled, flashing her tiny white teeth, and her mother mirrored the show of teeth. Their gazes broke as the husband turned abruptly away, shouldering through the crowd.

Felicia narrowed her eyes. "I'm so hungry. I'm going to eat three of everything."

"I asked you to change," the mother said, pushing the child from her. "The purple costume, I think. And put your hair up."

Tony circulated with his platter; he used the 'melding the salty and sweet' line, and the 'contrasting textures' line, again and again. The women at these parties liked to be seduced, he would tell me.

"The way a woman eats finger food says so much about her," he said. The women laughed. I still hadn't found the right way to talk to Lindsay, but I knew she'd have shuddered at this approach.

I circulated among the men; they plucked pieces from the tray without pausing their conversations, barely glancing at what they'd taken before putting it into their mouths and biting down. My shoes no longer squeaked as I walked, but my feet slid damply inside them.

Tony went out the back door to the deck to begin the next round of food, barbequed skewers. Several red-faced men had taken over the bar, and I washed glasses and platters, slipped through the room picking up discarded napkins and toothpicks.

The women spoke of the long hours their husbands worked, children's soccer, and the comparative merits of the people who cleaned their houses, trips to Rome they'd recently returned from. The men spoke of travelling for work, men's soccer, the expensive trips their wives wanted to take, and the boys-only golf trips they would earn by obliging. I moved among them, a salver with legs.

Tony waved at me from the glazed glass door to the deck. We plated and garnished stacks of chicken and shrimp skewers. Guests turned toward the aromas of citrus and satay, and Tony brushed past me into the crowd, platter held high.

The husband appeared with a stack of napkins. "Let's feed the kids."

The wide, polished wooden stairway doubled back on itself halfway up. I paused at the landing and looked down at the party. A woman was laughing, her hand on Tony's arm. The wife was momentarily still and unsmiling, her long fingers absently tracing a sharp hipbone as she watched her guests. A man glanced around before sliding his empty skewer onto the rim of a plant pot.

I stepped into the upper hallway, and the party noise disappeared: we entered a silence so thick, so heavy, a shiver ran over my skin. The hallway stretched empty before us, four doors opening off each side. I had seen at least five children enter this house with their parents, slipping away from them and up these stairs, as well as the little girl who lived here. But there was no sound or movement beyond my own audible breath.

"Kids, we have snacks," the husband called. There were scuffling sounds, and children appeared in every doorway. The movement and noise were immediate and overwhelming, erasing the void we'd stepped into seconds before.

They swarmed me, girls in sequined dresses, boys in cowboy and firefighter hats. Hands darted out, knocking at the platter. The husband laughed and gave out napkins.

His daughter examined the food but didn't take anything. A flash of emotion I didn't recognize crossed her father's face; his voice was harsh as he handed her a skewer. "You need to eat."

"I'm not hungry," she said, gazing up at him with wide, pained eyes. She glanced at me and smoothed her hands over the waist of her glittering purple dress. Its collar was a thick rhinestone choker high on her neck; from there it fell to a sleeveless V-shaped bodice that revealed skinny arms and the tops of her ribs; the purple sequins shot sparks as she swayed lightly from foot to foot. Her legs were long sticks under a short skirt made up of silvery-purple fringes. A silver rhinestone belt was slung low around her non-existent hips.

She nibbled daintily at the chicken, her eyes moving from his face to mine and back. As she ate, her arms caught the light and glittered with a fine silver dusting. Her long hair slipped into her food, and she tossed her head to clear it from her mouth. Her father wiped the sticky strands with a napkin; she stood patiently under his ministrations.

The children jostled my arms as they grabbed at second and third skewers, pulling me back into the busyness of their chatter and out of the odd pocket of stillness that had briefly surrounded Felicia, her father, and me. Empty skewers slid under my arms onto the rapidly emptying platter; a wooden stake jabbed at my hand, and I jumped, startled.

The other children disappeared again into various rooms, leaving the three of us in another abrupt, dizzying silence.

"Where did they come from?" I asked.

"We were in the walls," Felicia said.

The husband and Felicia led me then into her perfect pink bedroom and showed me the entrance hidden within her walk-in closet — miniature passages between the walls of the rooms and the outer walls of the house, a crawl space that didn't end. The tunnels wove behind hall and bedroom closets, wrapped around the end of the hall, a hidden maze wandering through the shadows of the upper floors.

"The rooms have false walls," the husband said. "We added extra insulation to deaden the sound, and now Felicia has a place for herself, kids only." He winked. "The only rooms not connected are the master bedroom and bath."

The tunnels were child-sized, four feet wide and about five feet tall — high enough for a child to walk upright, but not an adult. We stooped to peer in. Cave drawings littered the walls. "This is Felicia's space," the father said. "She does what she wants in here."

"I would have loved this when I was young," I said. Even now, I could barely resist diving in. To have a private space like this, the freedom to do what you wished without observation or judgement.

Felicia ran ahead, her legs flashing under the shimmering fringe of her skirt. "Come see."

The husband gestured me in but didn't follow. I took a cautious step, then another. Platter in hand, I hunched through the tunnels behind flickering purple sequins, ducking my head to avoid the low ceilings. Wall sconces hung every few feet, pockets of warmth alternating with pockets of dim mystery. Ahead of me, Felicia's dress sparkled then darkened as we moved in and out of shadows, around corners. Snatches of what looked like poetry or song lyrics were written on the walls. As I passed each pale yellow globe, and turned each corner, my shadow loomed and shrank again, disproportionate and unrecognizable.

Felicia disappeared around a corner, and for a moment I was caught in a pool of darkness between the lights, alone and with an oppressive feeling, as if the already close walls were narrowing around me. I clutched the platter to my chest and took three quick steps into the next swatch of light, where Felicia waited. My chest loosened again. A girl appeared from the dimness ahead. Her dance dress was blue with silver piping, too tight with a wide, short, netted skirt.

"Let's do our faces," Felicia said to her. They took the left fork, stepping over an abandoned doll with masses of silvery blonde ringlets: one blue eye was closed, the other wide, staring beyond my shoulder. Someone had scribbled a jagged black moustache on the doll's face and added exaggerated eyelashes that disappeared into its hairline.

I veered to the right. Three steps and their high-pitched laughter disappeared. The tunnel zigged and I found myself in the back of a closet. I stepped out, holding the platter to my chest to avoid smearing sauce on the linens. The husband waited for me in the hall.

"Amazing," I said. My chest thumped. I felt disoriented, as though I had stepped from one world into another.

"Every child needs a hiding place," he laughed without humour. "Sometimes it's necessary to escape your parents."

As I placed my foot on the top stair, the party noise from below resumed as though a switch had been flipped. My skin heated, a sharp contrast to how cool and damp my feet still were.

Tony waited for me on the deck, glaring as he slammed the lid closed on the barbeque. Black clouds loomed low and heavy, and the air was thick with unspent rain. Just out of my vision, the sky flickered with lightning; when I turned, it was gone.

"The children," I said, shrugging off Tony's look. We loaded more skewers on our platters, and I moved through the noisy, gossiping room until mine was empty. I retrieved the discarded skewer I'd watched the man hide in the plant pot, picked up crumpled napkins, waiting for the moment when I would again be summoned to climb the stairs.

I paused at the bottom of the stairs each time I passed. I couldn't hear a sound over the noise of the party, not a sign that there were children above me, moving silently in the walls, disappearing and reappearing at will. I wondered what they got up to in those dark hidden spaces — and what they would get up to when they were older.

The wife put her hand on my arm, and I jumped. "I hope you didn't let Felicia have too much," she said. "And nothing sticky."

I shook my head. "She was careful. She didn't get any on her dress."

"Her costume," she said. She stepped back into the party, smile brightening as she turned from me.

I cleaned up the most recent mess in the kitchen before piling the last of the skewers on a platter and looking at the husband. He nodded, and I climbed the stairs. The party sounds below disappeared again as I stepped into the hush of the upper hallway.

Two boys appeared from a half-sized cupboard, shattering the calm. "Fire! Everyone out."

I followed them to the pink room and peered in the closet. Felicia and the girl in the tight blue costume were on the floor in the tunnel, surrounded by brushes, tubes and jars of makeup, a lighted mirror beside them. One of the boys grabbed Felicia's arm. "Come with us. We're saving your lives."

She pulled free. "We don't have time to play. We're putting our faces on."

He shrugged and took a skewer from my platter. "Food!" he yelled. The others appeared. The food disappeared as rapidly as the first pile had.

I stepped cautiously back into the tunnels, shoulders hunched, arms outstretched with the remnants I had to offer. "More supper?"

Felicia shook her head. "I don't want to ruin my lipstick."

She tipped her face up to me, and three reflections in the lighted mirror did the same. She was made up, but not the way my cousins made themselves up when we were small, when I would watch them playing dress-up. Not like Lindsay and her friends, either, with their careless smudges of eyeliner or lip gloss. Felicia looked like a woman, eyes lined with shadows and glimmerings that made her pupils obsidian in the dim light. Her cheeks were soft angles and delicate glow. Her mouth a strawberry pout, wet and glistening. She smiled, showing her white teeth. In the mirror, multiple rows of Felicia's white teeth gleamed at me from multiple red mouths.

"Do I look pretty?"

"Very pretty."

"They used to use belladonna," she said, head tilted to meet my eyes.

"Belladonna?"

"To make a woman's eyes sparkle."

I nodded.

"They don't anymore because it's poison."

I nodded again.

"You'll want to take a picture of me," she said.

I set the platter on the floor and pulled my cell phone from my pocket. "Smile," I said.

She smiled. Her bizarrely adult eyes searched mine. She ran her fingers against her cheek to brush away a loose strand of hair, smoothed it into the thick mass that curved over her bare, sparkling shoulder. Her hand fell slowly across her chest. I clicked rapidly, barely looking at the screen on my phone. "There," I said, "all done." I slid my phone back into my pocket and bent to retrieve the platter I'd set at my feet. A skewer slipped to the edge of the tilting tray; I caught it with my fingers, pushed it back to safety.

Felicia turned to the girl in blue, tipping her face to one side, then the other as she examined her. "You need more lips and cheeks." She chose a brush, began applying colour to the girl's upturned face. She glanced back at me once, her black pupils swallowing the light. "I'm dancing later. You'll watch?"

"Of course."

I backed away from her shining red mouth, out of the tunnel. In her bedroom, full-length mirrors spanned one wall. A dozen pillows littered her bed, pink and white and red.

There were two skewers left on the platter. I bit into the first, ate it quickly, then the second, chewing and gulping so fast I didn't know if I was swallowing chicken or shrimp. Tony would fire me if he saw me eating their food. I wiped my mouth on a used napkin and descended the stairs. The party noise hit me like a wall, and I clenched the platter in shaking hands.

In the kitchen, Tony was removing the tenderloins from the bottom oven and placing them on a sideboard to rest. He raised his eyebrows. "The mother says her kid's going to put on a show. We'll serve the final course when she's done."

The wife drifted upstairs. When she returned, she paused halfway down the staircase, clapping her hands to get everyone's attention. She had brightened her own lipstick, and her mouth gleamed wet like her daughter's.

"Everyone, Felicia is about to do a routine for us. She won first place with it in her last dance competition."

People shifted to create a space in the centre of the room. The wife floated down the stairs, gesturing guests into corners, signalling to her husband to cue the music. He refused to meet her eyes, and she shrugged one thin shoulder, slid to the corner to do it herself. She flicked her hand at a man who hastened to move a standing lamp with a thick black base to the improvised dance floor.

I positioned myself with care at the kitchen sink: Tony would see me washing dishes whenever he checked, but I also had a clear view, between the shoulders of the guests, of the dance floor. Felicia descended the stairs slowly; her hand trailed along the banister, her smile trailed across everyone in the room. It rested on me, moved on. Her hair was now up in a loose, luxuriant bun at the top of her head, a glittering purple tiara encircling it. She took her place in the centre of the room, beside the lamp. The music began.

I was expecting the sort of music Lindsay likes, the Top 40 stuff DJs play in the bars she and her friends go to when they want to dance. But this was a jazz song, and Felicia sang along as she swayed through the room, her smile on high, her voice low. She twined around the lamp, offered her watchers sultry words of denial and desire. *I may say no, no, no. But do it again.*

I plunged my hands into the dishwater, blindly scrubbing at wineglasses and utensils. Felicia crumpled gracefully to the floor and folded in on herself. Tendrils from that mass of chocolate hair slipped out to caress her face, and she rose to blossom again. She caressed the thick lamp post and slid against it as she sang: *Mama may scold me, 'cuz she told me it was naughty, but then, oh, do it again.* She tossed her head; her mouth formed the red pout she'd shown me upstairs earlier. Strands of her loosened hair stuck to her glowing, moist lips. Her eyes glistened as if touched with Vaseline. I looked down at the sink.

The mother mouthed the words to the song, leaning toward her daughter with a fierce expression. The husband stood at the back of the room, arms crossed, staring from his wife to his daughter. The expression on his face took a moment to decipher: it looked like fear.

Felicia gave the room a heavy-lidded smile. She struck her final pose, cocking her hip, the fringes on her skirt parting around her thin thigh as she slid her little hands confidently down her flat chest. *Do it again.*

The mother rushed to the centre of the room and held her daughter's hand high; they bowed together as their audience clapped. A group of women clustered around them. "You must audition for that television show," they said. "She's certain to be famous."

Tony nodded at me, and I took the large knife from the cutting board. I sliced the rolled tenderloin with care to prevent the blue cheese stuffing from squeezing out. Red juices flowed from the meat beneath my hand and trickled into the deep grooves etched into the cutting board for just such a messy, sticky purpose. I sliced each piece to the same one-inch thickness, arranged them on separate platters for medium and rare. I rinsed the red from my hands and laid parsley at the edges of the plates.

Mother and daughter stood side by side, their faces mirrors, more so with the makeup. The resemblance ended, however, at their mouths: one brittle woman failing to look twenty, one little girl succeeding. I lowered my eyes again, set out individual serving plates and silverware.

The father walked forward and took Felicia's hand from her mother's. He inserted his body between them as he instructed her to wash her face and go play with her friends. She ignored him and came to me. I set the knife on the cutting board, so the sharp edge pointed away from her.

"Did you see me?"

"Very nice," I said. "Well done." The words sounded ridiculous even as I spoke them, and her black shining eyes laughed as if we shared a joke. Through the glass doors to the deck, a jagged fork of lightning split the sky. Thunder followed seconds later. The partygoers didn't pause in their conversation. I busied myself handing plate after plate of rare meat to Tony, as ordered. The fringes of Felicia's skirt brushed my leg as she moved away.

Tony and I laid out fruit, cheese, and tarts, washed and dried dishes and glassware and repacked them, each in its designated spot with its designated wrapper. The rain thrummed against the deck door and the roof as we worked. My back throbbed from bending over the sink.

I looked up the stairs each time I passed. No sound penetrated the invisible wall at the top of the staircase, and yet I was more aware of the secret life unfolding above me than the one I observed on the main floor. I slipped out the back door carrying the last tub, felt my feet slide in the mud on the driveway. The rain had stopped again, and the night was deep and shining, filled with the last patters of raindrops releasing from the trees.

Tony held out his hand, and I flinched. "The kid said you dropped this."

It was my phone. I hadn't known I'd lost it. I slid it into my pocket, slammed the back doors to the van. My foot slid against a cluster of wet leaves ripped from the trees by the storm, and I lost my balance, coming up hard against the back of the van. My phone slid from my pocket again, clattering against the hitch on the bumper before bouncing into a shallow puddle. I cursed and grabbed for it, wiping it against my pants. I zipped it into a deep jacket pocket for safety. We drove to the restaurant. More unloading and putting away.

I had been invited to join Lindsay and her friends at a bar tonight. The invitation was casual, thrown out as an afterthought as I lingered at the edges of the conversation. I had planned to go, but now I was unsettled. My back was a series of tiny, flaming knots, and my thigh had begun to throb from falling against the bumper.

It was after midnight when I got into my car. My phone lit up as I pulled it from my jacket and brushed the screen. The image was all wrong. The photo I took of Felicia inside the upstairs walls had been set as my screen saver. The darkness of the tunnel loomed behind her, carving shadows into her cheeks and deepening her eyes to black. The screen had smashed when my phone struck the truck's metal hitch. Felicia's image was cracked; the point of impact began at the top left corner in that unnaturally thick hair and spiderwebbed down, pausing here and there to pinpoint and reflect a shoulder, a wrist, a dusting of glitter on her cheeks. Black and silver fissures traced and separated her eyes, a deep split zagging to her full red lips. Her face darkened again as my phone went to sleep and I ran my thumb over the activate button again. I traced my fingers over her smiling, shattered face, felt the cracks beneath my dishwater hands.

I shook my head, and scrolled back to older photos, looking for one I had taken of Lindsay months ago. She didn't know I'd taken it — she was sitting in the cafeteria with her friends, head back as she laughed. I'd held my phone at table height, pretending to text while I snapped five fast tilting shots. Later I'd gone through them, deleting the fuzzy ones. I cropped the best one to zoom in on her face. As usual, Lindsay wore little or no makeup; her dirty blonde hair was pulled back into a messy bun, blending with the beige institutional wall behind her. Now the cracked screen etched lines across her face, aging her; her pale, laughing mouth receded infinitesimally as I stared at the screen.

My thumb stroked the surface and Felicia came at me again through the cracks, straining to break through; the shadows of her dark eyes and the red of her mouth glowing in the car's dim interior, taking me back to the deep shadow and light of the tunnels. She had sent me away with many photos, I saw now. Close-ups of wall drawings and scrawls I hadn't seen in my brief explorations of those hidden spaces, and I thumbed through them all, straining to make out the faces and the words before shoving my phone back in my pocket and starting the car.

I drove to my apartment, hands trembling on the wheel. I steered hard through puddles that threatened to yank my tires from their forward course. I muttered to myself as I wrenched at the wheel, hardly knowing where I was going. Steam rose from the glistening streets, and my tires hissed against the pavement. My phone pulsed in my pocket.

I kicked my apartment door closed against the night, heart pounding as I sank into a chair for a closer study of the images Felicia had sent me away with.

A pot of purple glitter spilling onto the floor in a pool of light cast by a sconce, the plush darkness just beyond. A high heeled woman's shoe edging out of the frame, casting long shadows against a secret wall. A cave drawing, scratched out in pink glitter pen, that looked vaguely like me — the cowlick at my right temple, the squint of my eyes: I looked alarmed. In another, a naked Barbie sprawled where she'd been thrown into a shadowed corner. A scratch on the wall above her long, splayed legs indicated she'd met its surface with force; her blonde hair had been roughly chopped off and the uneven stubble jutted out from her head at jarring angles; dark pen scribbles peeked from between her legs and a tiny plastic bandage covered the ubiquitous Barbie smile. More images: Felicia's full, unsmiling mouth. A single dark eye that glistened as though anointed with belladonna. There was a reflection in the pupil — a figure I couldn't quite make out.

Mystery barista

It's important to look pensive, but not sullen — it's a fine line, but, if you've learned anything from creeping his Twitter feed, it's that he will notice if you cross it. Rather, @freerangedreamer will withdraw his notice if you cross it. Likewise, you have to use your hair, but you can't make it look like you're using your hair. That one's tricky — hair play works on most men, regardless of the degree of finesse employed. Dreamers, though, are a different story. They track any overuse of the subliminal or seductive gesture and become immediately disinterested, turning their gazes to the skinnier, paler women huddled next to windows. Perhaps it's just as well that, in your role as @freerangedreamer's barista, you are forced to be subtle because you can't touch your hair — health regulations and all that.

Tuesday afternoon, as you were cleaning tables around him, you happened to glance at his laptop and saw his Twitter handle. That night you looked him up; he is always pleasant, a good tipper. To your surprise, you saw yourself. You didn't see him; his avatar is a grey painting of a man, back to the viewer, walking through pelting rain. But this tweet must be about you — it appeared this afternoon:

Her thoughts are far away as she cleans around me; she smiles through her exhaustion . . . present, yet unknowable #MysteryBarista

You see tweets about other strangers — other women — @freerangedreamer has encountered. There are regulars, but this is the first time you recognize yourself.

Now, you turn your head casually, pretending to look out the window, so that your long glossy ponytail falls forward over your shoulder. There, that's very good. You lift your head to gaze around the room, a farseeing sort of gaze, as though you are replaying a pivotal moment in your head rather than seeing the people around you.

This awareness of being watched has changed the way you interact with customers, at least while the dreamer is in the coffee shop. You speak in lower tones, with less animation. This creates a striking contrast for the rare occasion when you let yourself laugh out loud. His head swivels when you do, and you eagerly search his feed that night. He describes your laugh as a bell-like sound, an unexpected moment of purity in a drab day. Same hashtag.

When he asks your favourite drink, you are prepared. You have a weakness for frothy coffee and whipped cream concoctions with caramel drizzled on top, but you know they are not the right choice — these are not serious drinks, not befitting an enigma. You have read his tweets, seen how easily he gets bored and moves on to another subject. Tea, you tell him. Lapsang souchong, or a steamed Darjeeling. And in the evenings, you say, red wine. You're proud of the red wine detail — you added it at the last minute, on the fly. But in your own reading — and your observations at art print stores in the mall — it seems men are more drawn to a red wine drinking, pensive woman than a white wine drinker with the same expression. And, in these watching situations, brunettes finally have the advantage. It helps to look mistily tired, too.

That night you are amazed to realize that #MysteryBarista has begun to gather steam — other men are now using it too. Some have photos on their profiles, and their observations are less than acute. Others, like the dreamer, are more eloquent behind their symbolic renderings. The feed under #MysteryBarista runs the gamut from *She works hard for the money* to photos of baristas taken without their knowledge. They all conjure what their mystery baristas' homes smell like — some are perfumed, some smell of comfort food. Your dreamer seems to envision you frozen in some kind of Flashdance pose, knees under your chin, wearing pliable clothing.

You can't believe this. It reminds you of when you were twenty, when you finally got that stalker you'd always wanted. How delicious the slow realization that he was everywhere you were, that his gaze never left you. Your girlfriends were shocked and thrilled. When he placed a note on your car, saying he'd left a present on your doorstep, you were terrified he had killed your landlady's cat. Even as you raced home, your spine crawled with awe — to be the object of such passion, such single-minded devotion. To think, of all the girls who'd paraded across his gaze, of all those who had vied for his attention, you were the one to land his contemplation. You were deeply relieved to find the cat alive, but the carnation bouquet was anticlimactic. Shortly after, your stalker got a transfer; he left another note on your car that he was moving away.

But this — this is better. And to think you'd never have known if you hadn't peered over his shoulder at his laptop screen. You never would have been alerted to start wearing slightly darker eyeliner, slightly paler makeup. You suspect the dreamer is too much of a romantic to take a photo unknown to you, but it's always wise to be prepared. You've slacked off on your appearance in the year since the musician wandered away.

This relationship with the dreamer is different from the musician. Initially, with the musician, you believed you wanted love. You laugh now to think of it — love! What's important is to be in service to a higher ideal. The bonus, of course, is that it's not a full-time job. You are picked up and set down, left with plenty of time to pursue whatever it is women like you pursue when you aren't being watched.

When the musician left you, night after night, to stay late and practise with the band, it was in the service of his art. More heroic still were the sacrifices of touring. Occasionally, he wrote a song about your patience, as a reward. You sounded beautiful in these songs, valiant, even saintly. Women loved to hear him sing about you; it made them press their bodies against this haunted, complicated man, which led him to write more haunted, complicated songs. You were like a mother waving her little boy off for his first day of school. He couldn't wait to leave, as long as he knew you were watching him go, yearning for him to return, anxious to hear and applaud his stories of adventure. And the subtleties he taught you are helpful now, as you walk from behind the counter to wipe tables and gather empty coffee cups.

As you approach the dreamer, you let your gaze drift past him, allow a small flicker — regret, perhaps, or is it sorrow? — to cross your face and disappear again in a moment. You see him watching you out of the corner of his eye. You need to be careful here; the slightest wrong move, and he could slip away. You lift your chin to look out the window, and then the pièce de résistance: you rub your temple — just the right touch of weariness, and — yes! — all without smudging your makeup.

His eyes slide over you, his fingers slip to his keyboard, stroke the keys softly. That night you read that he sees you've been hurt. And misunderstood.

You are thrilled.

You plan how tomorrow you will run a slow, absentminded finger under your scoop necked shirt, sliding your slipping bra strap back to your shoulder. You will wear your high black boots. It's a delicate balance — presenting attractiveness and hauntedness in equal proportions — but you're confident you can pull it off, send his mind from the easy path of your sexuality down the more nuanced trail of imagining how the men in your life couldn't match that sexuality, were threatened by it, or some related mental swagger.

And his mind does wander there, and his online observations follow. He is quite poetic, your dreamer. And he is not alone; all across Twitter, reams of men dream of soothing broken, naked serving women under the hashtag #MysteryBarista.

The next day, you call in sick; the element of surprise is important to keeping any relationship fresh. You spend the day eating chocolate or reading romance novels, or the other secret rituals that women like you do. And, the day after that, you tell your boss you have to leave early — an appointment, you say. You wait until the dreamer has settled into his usual chair with his usual dark roast before you remove your apron and step out from behind the counter.

As you pull on your jacket, you close your eyes in a long, slow blink, as if girding yourself for what awaits you. You fumble with your sleeve in such a way that your back arches, just for a second. Then you remove your ponytail holder and shake out your hair. Lower your voice to a husky, accidentally audible murmur when you say to your colleague behind the counter: wish me luck. Toss it off as you head for the door, so he has no time to show confusion. The words, after all, are meant for the dreamer, not for him.

The dreamer will remain in the coffee shop for another hour after you leave, pounding down words of you, of what he knows about you. He recognizes you, and that's got to be the most important acknowledgement that's happened to you in ages. And then he'll go home and climb on his girlfriend, or his wife, because these men who dream of coffee shop women generally already have women in their lives — women who are too familiar, women who hold no more surprises. He'll hammer into this predictable, non-hashtag-worthy woman with his eyes closed, dreaming of you and your broken, haunted hashtag eyes. He will fall away from her, joyous and heaving, hopeful that his words will finally reveal the complexity of your existence.

And those words of his — you're hoping for a poem, or a story. You know it's coming. And who knows, maybe #MysteryBarista will even trend on Twitter. In the meantime, you'll sit here, in a trance, waiting to be observed again. As you wait, your thin sweater is slipping off your shoulder. Maybe tomorrow you'll break a glass, perhaps even slice a non-essential finger as he watches you gather the shards.

Not the apocalypse I was hoping for

It's a good thing I wasn't able to set up my phone so I could film myself kicking in the door, since, apparently, I'm not man enough to actually kick in the stupid door. Jesus, this is annoying. By the third kick, I'm putting everything into it, planting my combat boot at the doorframe right below the lock, as square as I can. The door's thicker than it looked from the street, a big green resistant wooden slab. I pull an Adirondack chair over and hold on to it for balance, using my right foot as a battering ram — one, two, three, four. Every kick jars me all the way through my hipbone, and still that motherfucker won't give. I lose my balance on five and land on my ass against a flowerpot on the deck, dirt and orange and pink petals splattering all over me. That would've looked great on social media, real graceful.

My legs are shaking. I dust off the dirt and flower bits and look around until I find a black metal side gate that leads to the back yard. The wind shifted this morning, and the air in this otherwise perfect neighbourhood is thick with the stench of the buildings that are burning on the other side of the city — the biggest campfire in the world, topped with an added reek of plastics and chemicals and all the other crap that houses are made of now.

I poke around in an unlocked shed, coughing so hard I can barely catch my breath, find an axe. I march back to the front door and swing the axe again and again at the same spot on the green doorframe, cursing this and every other fancy house on Larch Crescent, my hair falling salty and stinging into my eyes.

My arms ache, and I can't stop coughing, but I keep swinging through it, like a big, sweating, enraged machine — like Orlando Bloom in *Kingdom of Heaven*, all righteous and furious and bloodied. I'm so angry now, so focused on hacking the shit out of the door frame, I forget to keep an eye out for cops or firefighters. When the door finally cracks and splinters, I use my boot again. This time the bitch gives way. In movies, the goddamn door always gives, if not on the first booted kick, then on the second.

I go straight to the bathroom, bent over with the force of my hacking, looking for cough syrup in the cabinet, under the sink. Nothing. I catch sight of myself in the mirror — hair sweaty and lank, smudges on my face, my hands, my clothes. I look like Bruce Willis halfway through *Diehard*. I laugh; Brittany Frigid Malone wouldn't think I was a pussy if she saw me now. Yippee-ki-yay, motherfucker Malone.

I head back to the kitchen and pull a glass from a cupboard, fill it with ice water from the fridge dispenser and chug it. My throat eases up enough for me to plug in my phone and explore the rest of the house. No cough drops to be found in the entire house, and I can't find any booze, either, other than half a bottle of fruit wine in the fridge. Who the fuck lives like this? But at least my phone's charging. The power went out on my side of town but — big surprise — the lights are still on in the rich neighbourhood. That's why I chose this house — their motion sensor lit up when I walked up the sidewalk. That, and their wooden door looked easier to spring than some of its neighbours — at least, it did from the sidewalk, through the haze and my watering eyes.

Maybe I didn't think this through, but tell me how you'd do any better. The government started whimpering about evacuating the city because the fires were getting too close, and my first response was: fuck that, the government is a bunch of old ladies. This is my city, and no one's going to tell me I have to leave. I know what happens in disasters: people start out heroic, but it doesn't take long for the losers to crawl out of the woodwork.

By the time it was clear the fire was moving toward the easternmost neighbourhoods, by the time they'd announced the voluntary/mandatory evacuation, whatever the fuck that means, I'd come up with my own plan. I created a Twitter account called @NorhavenFireWatch, with a hashtag to match. I went to the edge of the city and snapped a bunch of photos with my cell phone: the lit-up woods puking out black spirals into the orange and grey sky, the fire licking at the edges of town. My avatar is a death-of-civilization sky filled with flames and smoke. When the police went door to door asking everyone to leave, I just smiled and nodded, same as I did with my parents.

I waved my mom and dad off, said I'd be on the road soon, too, but I had to pack a few last things — I told them I was heading east instead of south, to stay with a buddy. I swear, I had to promise my mother sixteen times that I would actually leave.

There was so much confusion, all those freaked out people flooding to the exit points. I climbed the bluff on the west side of the city and got some good shots of that long snaking line of vehicles, all with their lights on, colourless apparitions against this great backdrop of glowing red treetops against soft dark pillows of smoke. I texted my parents the next day, said I'd made it to my buddy's and was having a cold one, glued to the news just like everyone else.

I'm here to document it all: the fire, and what goes on in a supposedly abandoned city. You can't trust the people who say they're here to protect you, and I'm here to hold them accountable — to be a citizen watchdog. By the second day of the evacuation, I had over eight hundred followers. People used my hashtag to talk about the fire. I had dozens of shares, replies, and requests to post more pics.

I'd been snapping photos almost randomly, because how could you go wrong with such an amazing sky? But as the comments rolled in, and my followers grew, I started to take more time, cropping, adding filters to make the oranges and reds brighter. The smoke took over the sky — it blocked the sun in great billows — dozens of shades of light and dark greys, the bright flames pushing through in flickering waves. The sky pushed ash and campfire stench into the city until fire was all you could think about, even dream about. And as the citizens poured out in a panicked, choking stream, the fire crews, police, helicopters, and air tankers poured in. I'm especially proud of a shot I took of a military-looking chopper against a fierce orange and black sky. That one got shared almost two thousand times.

Needless to say, that level of photography and posting drains the phone battery fast. I needed to charge it twice a day, and, I have to admit, I didn't think about how I'd manage that when the electricity went out. I didn't think about losing wi-fi either, but that hasn't happened. Good old satellites.

The first few days, I idled my car in the garage and used my car charger — the man door cracked open so I wouldn't die, of course — out of sight of roving police and firefighters. But then something weird started to happen. People started tweeting me to ask me to check their houses: someone was worried their house had been broken into; someone else wasn't sure they'd locked their doors. One woman had set up a lawn sprinkler on her roof, and she asked me to go turn it on if the fire seemed to be moving to that corner of the city. I didn't do that one, because the water pressure in the city was shit, and I didn't want to bring attention to my activities. But suddenly I was doing all these drive-bys, checking doors and windows, posting photos of people's houses so they'd know everything was okay. My follower numbers were shooting through the roof.

A man asked me to feed his fish. He DMed me to say where he'd hidden his spare house key. I went in and fed his fish, posted a photo of my hand shaking food into the water and the fat goldfish burbling up to gasp and gobble at the surface.

I didn't mention that I ate a bag of ripple chips while I was doing it. It's a small price to pay for the life of his fish, right? I mean, I was taking a risk driving around, considering I wasn't supposed to be in the city, and police were looking for those of us they described as 'non-compliant.' But I've been roaming these streets and alleys for twenty-one years, I know how to avoid the cops.

A few people asked me to look for their dogs, and I thought how cool it would be to find one of those roaming dogs and travel together through this apocalypse. A cool dog, like that French bulldog in *Armageddon* — Little Richard was the dog's name — who fights some dude on the street for a toy while asteroids are crashing into the earth.

I blew up on Twitter within hours of the fish bit. Eight-thousand-plus followers, including some media asking me to do interviews — no thanks, that's not what anonymous soldiers do — and a shitload of retweets. Girls started asking how old I was, what I looked like. One girl tweeted that she'd give me a gratitude blowjob once the fires were out. I pulled up her profile picture, but it was one of those extreme closeups, and it was hard to tell if she was hot. Probably not. Hot girls usually use photos that show off their looks, and they don't generally publicly offer blowjobs to strangers. I replied with an LOL. Never hurts to keep your options open, right?

So, I was suddenly a hero. And not just a hero, but a #hero. But my car was down to an eighth of a tank and I was using it up fast, driving around town doing chores for a bunch of strangers. And every gas station in town had been drained during the evacuation.

But I'm enterprising, which is why I knew I'd be fine staying behind, documenting this goddamn disaster, owning this fucking town, when everyone else gave in and left.

I didn't have a choice, breaking into these houses. But what's a bit of damage compared to the peace of mind I'm giving so many people? Insurance will cover a couple of broken doors or windows. These are people living in limbo, not sure if their house and all their treasured possessions have been eaten by the monster fire. They're counting on me to soothe their fears, and I can't do that if my phone's dead. But I did figure at least a few people would be in such a hurry that they wouldn't lock their houses — that I'd be able to get in somewhere and charge my phone. Even the woman who begged me to check her house because she was so worried she'd left it open had locked it up safe and tight. That was a disappointment. Whatever happened to the days of trusting your neighbour?

I thought about siphoning gas from other cars, so I could keep driving around to take care of all the requests and charge my phone at the same time. Maybe siphoning gas was easier in the good old days, but even if I'd wanted to suck the gas up like Cheech did in *Up in Smoke* — or was that Chong? — new vehicles don't work that way. I tried to pry open the fuel flap on two different cars, not that I had a hose anyway, but I figured I'd deal with that once I got into a gas tank in the first place. Both times ended up with the cars honking and blinking, and me racing away looking over my shoulder for cops.

So, breaking into this big, fancy, landscaped house was necessary. I was desperate. Now, while my phone is finally charging, I can stop and catch my breath. Larch Crescent is a quiet loop, so no one's going to drive by; having said that, it's one of the more expensive areas, so maybe police patrol it more.

And they'll see right away that the front door of the house has been chopped up. I walk back out to the porch. I set the flowerpot straight and tuck the axe behind it, straighten the toppled chair. I'd forgotten there was a screen door; once I swing it closed, the damage to the door is harder to see. Just in case, though, I unplug my phone from the kitchen counter and head to the rear of the house to the master bedroom.

I'm coughing less now that I've calmed down. But, Jesus, when this is over, I don't know if I'll ever be about to sit around a campfire again.

I check the massive bathroom off the master bedroom again for cough syrup or candies. Nope. What the fuck is it with people? Don't they have kids they have to think of? Every fucking kid I know is a walking bag of germs — don't these people plan ahead?

The bedroom has double glass doors that lead to a back deck — perfect. I plug my phone into the wall, crack the glass doors and peer out. The streets are still. The wind has shifted again and cleared off some of the smoke, so I can see the hills at the edge of town, newly bare of trees. I close the doors again and head back to the kitchen to grab the fruit wine from the fridge. I settle on the edge of the bed. The comforter is pale brown with silver thread running through it, and I laugh to think about the filthy, wild Bruce Willis clone I saw in the mirror, how we're dirtying this pretty room. Yippee-ki-yay, motherfuckers, I say, and take a swig. It's sweet and thick, and my lips immediately feel sticky. I take another drink, start going through the bedside tables. I've got an hour to kill before my phone is fully charged.

To be honest, all these chores for strangers are getting boring — I mean, I want to help, that's why I stayed. But it's one thing to take great photos and report on the fire to allay people's fears — that's a reason for them to call me #hero. Not sure how heroic it is, though, to do chores for them — especially the same menial chores over and over. I don't water the lawn for my parents; why should I do this shit for strangers? And the people who want me to check on their pets? I'm all, why the fuck didn't you take them with you? I can see not taking the goldfish. But what kind of asshole leaves four-legged pets to burn up in a fire?

In the second bedside table, I find the porn magazines. Nice. I punch up the pillows against the headboard and lie on the bed, leafing through them. The guy who lives here is clearly a breast man, there's a lot of silicone in these pages.

I drink more wine. What I really need on this adventure is a hot chick sidekick. Like that hot, tough girl who linked up with Woody Harrelson and that small dude with the big hair in *Zombieland*, and then it was the smaller, normal guy who ended up getting into her pants.

Or someone like this blonde with the shaved pussy. Maybe she's trapped in a house when the fire suddenly changes direction. No one knows she's there, because, like me, she stayed behind and hid from police. And now the fire is licking at her house and the smoke is overwhelming her and she can't get out. She's terrified. When I break through the door with two solid kicks, she's cowering in the running shower, hoping the water will save her from the flames. Her long, wet hair is pushed back behind her ears, and the tiny white dress she's wearing is completely transparent, her huge nipples are dark through the wispy fabric. She gasps when she sees me, her eyes wide and grateful, her face streaked with mascara. She clings to me as I carry her from the house. As I run, her hard nipples press against my chest, and when she shifts to clutch me closer, my hand accidentally moves under her short dress, and she isn't wearing underwear. I race to another house down the street that's out of the fire's swath and carry her inside, my hand brushing against her hot grateful thighs. I lay her down on a bed. She won't let go of me. She pulls me down with her. My hero, she murmurs, you saved my life. Then, just like the magazine spread I'm looking at, her fingers peel up her dress and she starts touching herself where she's smooth and wet and pink.

I'm rubbing myself through my jeans. I sit up and take another gulp of wine, then head to the bathroom clutching the magazine in one hand and unzipping my jeans with the other. I'd rather do it on these people's soft, plushy bed, but I'm not going to leave my cum all over their comforter — DNA and all that.

After, my coughing is worse. I'm doubled over on the toilet, jeans around my ankles, barking up a lung. I wonder if the regular exposure to smoke is doing permanent damage to me. I've generally been staying on the safe side of the city, but yesterday I went into the areas that are burning at the east end of the city. I got some amazing wreckage photos, and it was incredible being in the danger zone, ducking and weaving to avoid the firefighters and all the military-looking equipment. At one point, there were flaring red embers and still-warm ashes falling on me, and I just had to stop and stare, try to get photos and catch them on my hand, like some little kid in the freakiest snowstorm ever. I wore a painter's mask I'd found in yet another unlocked shed, but I don't know now if that was enough: my throat has been raspy and raw all day.

I straighten myself out, grab my phone, and pull my T-shirt up over my mouth and nose. I slip out through the deck doors and down the alley; my car is parked two blocks away, snug against the garage door in someone's driveway, so it looks like it belongs.

It's weird driving through a deserted city, eyes going in all directions looking for cops or firefighters, looking for other signs of life, taking side streets and alleys to my parents' house. I breathe relief as I duck inside and sit on the floor in the kitchen, where I can't be seen from the front windows or door. The fire shifted away from my neighbourhood the other day, but the electricity is still off.

My phone lights up the minute I sit down — a text from my mother. Are you sure you're okay, blah blah blah. Asking me all these tricky little questions like she doesn't believe I actually left town. I scroll through my phone and send her a pic I took a few months ago, drinking beer with a buddy she's never met. Yeah, Ma, me and Craig are doing fine, just chilling, waiting for it to be over. And my fucking mother texts back and says, wow, your hair's grown a lot in the last week.

I flip her off and go to my home screen. I was planning to google the effects of smoke inhalation, but I've got a shitload of notifications; I haven't checked Twitter in hours, what with my phone dying again overnight and then the hours it took to break into that fucking house and charge the damn phone. I'm eager to see what people are saying — I'm really happy with the photos I posted yesterday. It took me a while to come up with the right sympathetic tweets to go with them, because, frankly, it was stellar. Trees with one side burned to a crisp, the other side green and leafy — that's how fast the fire blew through some areas, like a tornado, decimating select parts and leaving others whole before sweeping on to its next target. Piles of smoldering ash, and weird pieces of wreckage like a blackened bike frame, or a bald doll, or a cast iron frying pan sitting intact in a heap of twisted kitchen appliances. As a backdrop, more houses with their roofs on fire, destined to become ash themselves. And as a backdrop to all that, the huge, apocalyptic sky.

I've earned hundreds of hits, and even more replies. I scroll quickly, but some of the responses don't make sense on their own; it looks like there are a whole bunch of threads. I go back to the top and start following the rabbit trail of conversations and spin-off conversations and arguments that spiderweb off on their own tangents.

Fuck, people aren't happy with the wreckage photos. A few do love them, but they're a solid minority who aren't from Norhaven, and they've been out-yelled by everyone else in the world.

Some bitch named Chloe, who evacuated with the other sheep, is calling me insensitive, saying a random photo from some guy on social media is no way for people to find out they've lost everything. She literally retweeted every one of my wreckage photos with snotty comments about the guy behind them, wondering who I was, and what kind of shit I was getting up to in her supposedly abandoned city. She didn't call me some guy, though. She called me some douche.

That pissed me off, and I tweeted her back, saying, we all know where a douche is supposed to go — in your twat.

I mean, seriously? Here I am, endangering myself to help people, and she has the nerve to criticize me from the safety of her air-conditioned hotel room?

I click on the hashtag, and there's more. How did I miss this? For two days now, some guy named Brendon has also been tweeting from Norhaven, using #NorhavenFireWatch, MY hashtag. Fucking Brendon is a firefighter, he looks like he oiled himself up and did pushups before taking his profile selfie. He's getting lots of requests from people about their houses too, and he's checking them on the few hours he has off from fighting the fires, reporting back like some guy from CNN. Fucking Brendon is also warning them not to trust strangers with their personal information. He's basically warning them against me while using my hashtag, the fucker. Like he's not a stranger, too. But he's a firefighter, ooh. And Jesus, really? Here's a photo of him holding a puppy he rescued last night. It's got more than fifty-six hundred shares, and it's only been up for a couple of hours. Jesus, this fucker is going viral — all thanks to my idea — and he's bashing me at the same time. Firefighters are such glory whores.

I can't fucking believe this. Through the kitchen window, the sky flickers with choking plumes of black and yellow. Two helicopters buzz low above the abandoned shopping centre a couple of blocks away. I grab a bottle of water and the flashlight; I grope my way downstairs to the basement in the dark before turning it on as I walk into my bedroom. I'm not sure what to do other than sink down on my bed and close my eyes. I lie there trying to calm down, but I can't — I swing my legs around to sit back up and I punch my pillow again and again. I kick at my desk and chair with both feet until they topple against the far wall.

The exertion aggravates my throat, and I start coughing again. I drop the flashlight trying to get the water bottle open; it bounces across the floor, and I leave it there. I pull my phone back out and reread some of the bullshit accusations against me. Opportunistic? Dangerous idiot? Hero complex? Looter? What the fuck do these goddamn armchair psychologists know?

At some point I fall asleep, and I startle awake again after a couple of hours. My phone is on my chest, and I shove it into my pocket without looking. I can't sit here in the dark in the basement of my parents' house; I'll lose my shit. I run through friends in my mind, think about which ones have parents who like to drink. And who'll have food options — I'm starving. Jason's parents don't live too far from me, but it's far enough that they're in the electricity zone. I haven't been there since he moved out a couple of years ago, but if I remember right, I should be able to break a little pane of glass in their back door to get in.

The light is dull as I walk to Jason's house; this time of year it doesn't get dark until eleven, but the sun is hidden behind a shifting wall of smoke. There seem to be more police cars than earlier, and I do a lot of melting behind trees and fences and abandoned cars. Jason's back door is how I remember it, and I pull the ball-peen hammer from my pocket and lightly smash the glass closest to the lock. I've seen this done a million times in movies. Once I break it, I run the hammer handle around the frame to clear out the jagged pieces of glass. I reach in and unlock the door and I'm in, as slick as if I'd been born to a life of crime. Now this would've made a nice video clip for all those assholes.

One hand is on the fridge door and the other wrapped around a bottle of Jason's dad's rum when I hear the clunk of boots coming up the front steps. Fuck. I dive behind the kitchen island just before the cop rings the doorbell. I twist my head around to see if I'd been dumb enough to turn the light on, and that's when I realize I'm trapped: my fucking hoodie snagged on the stupid frilly silver knob of Jason's mother's oversized pots and pans drawer when I ducked out of sight, and I can't move my head — my face is smashed up against the trendy dark wood of the island. I'm twisted enough so I can't reach around to free my hood with my left arm. I can't use my right, because my elbow will jut up above the island, and the cop will see it through the bevelled glass door with the little red and purple glass insets Jason's stupid mother thought was classy. I can't even maneuver to take a swig from the rum bottle while I'm trapped here.

The cop's radio squawks, and he mutters into it. The worst part is trying not to cough — my eyes water from the effort to hold it back. Naturally, the cop is going to lean on the doorbell for five goddamn minutes while I die quietly in here. I twist my body around to pull my knees further out of sight and try to work up saliva so I can swallow and soothe my raw throat. My cell phone digs into my hipbone. I haven't shaved in days, and my stubble is being shoved back into my pores by the wood panelling I'm mashed up against. Who the fuck needs a house this big anyway, with all these goddamn pantries and drawers? They only have one kid, and he doesn't even live here anymore.

What if the cop sees me and decides to act like one of those cops who are all over the news blindly firing at unarmed people every week? My heart pounds as loud and hard as the cop going at the door. I can see his long shadow across the floor, feel his eyes lasering into the room through those stained-glass insets.

This is not one of my more tweetable moments, cowering behind this ridiculous kitchen island. So not cool or #heroic. I choke back another dry cough and keep my eyes glued to the cop's shadow. Jason's mother sure wasn't worried about peeping Toms or stalkers — they might as well post a video above their door showing what they're doing — that's how hard it is to hide behind all the glass in this stupid, open-concept home.

The cop yells, "Negative" to another cop who's making a similar noise at the house next door, and that's when I realize it's a woman. Her boots clump off the porch, and I breathe out, hacking into my shirt as quietly as I can. I unhook myself from the knob and slither across the floor to peer out at the street. Jesus, she's an Amazon. Nearly six feet tall, her blonde hair in a low lady-cop bun, striding down the street to the next house, barking ten codes into her radio through the mask over her face. Even through the chunky uniform I can see she's totally fucking buff, and she strides along like she's starring in some chick action movie. Taller than the dude she's walking with, too. The lady cop makes this weird jerking off gesture, and they laugh.

My throat explodes, and I run to the back of the house so they won't hear. I unscrew the top from the rum and chug it down, spilling it over my chin and shirt. That makes me cough in a different way and tears stream out of my eyes, but I don't give a fuck. I hunker down on Jason's mother's floral couch, wish I could turn on Jason's dad's big screen TV. Instead, I drink for half an hour, then get up and dig around the kitchen. I pull a bag of Oreos from the cupboard and alternate — a cookie, a drink, back and forth. Then I pull out my phone and see that my life as a hero is completely over-the-top dead and fucked.

Who the fuck knew people could activate their home security videos remotely? Some guy is complaining because I told him I'd checked his house, but he checked his video and saw that I hadn't been there. And — fuck, this is bad — the owners of the brown and silver comforter also have video. In their bedroom. Right now they're saying they won't post any photos of me lying on their bed reading a skin magazine and rubbing my cock, because, you know, taste and NSFW and all that shit. But they're pissed, and they're going to give the video to the cops. And the hate being poured on me from all corners of the Twitterverse is truly stunning. I can barely stand to keep reading after I see how they've bastardized my hashtag to #NorhavenDickWatch. It's trending locally.

The whole city is laughing at me, plus thousands of random strangers who have nothing better to do than dance on other people's misfortune online. The lady cop's jerk-off motion and laughter make total sense now — the cops weren't just doing another check. They were looking for me, specifically.

To top it all off, the feminists have leapt all over me for my douche/twat comeback to that bitch Chloe. I'm fucking dead. Or I would be, if they knew who I was. I drink more rum and try to calm myself down. They don't know who I am. But my heart keeps hammering at my chest, because some smartass could figure it out if they tried. Plus, the cops have the video, and they're probably going to splash my face all over the net, asking people to ID me. And women are screaming hate at me, calling me a tiny-dicked porn-loving misogynist. Jesus. I power my phone down and concentrate on drinking. The Oreos do not taste good.

I know it's dumb, but I feel like there's an angry mob waiting for me outside Jason's mother's house. I tiptoe to the front door and peer out. The street is empty. And then I see the dog trotting down the middle of the road, looking purposeful.

I step out onto the porch. Finally, I say, there you are. I wave the bottle of rum at him and whistle. The dog looks at me but doesn't slow down or change his course. Come on, boy, I say, we've got to stick together, like sidekicks, right? It's a fucking apocalypse.

I mean, the dog can't open closets to get at his kibble, right? Or use a can opener to get at cold canned spaghetti. He should be scared, abandoned by his jackass owners in this stinking, smoking town, watching the flames jumping from tree to tree and licking at the north subdivisions. He should be overjoyed to see a man who can save him.

But no. The dog looks at me like I'm a piece of shit on the bottom of his paw and keeps loping down the street like he'll be better off on his own. He's a mutt, for fuck's sake. Black with a couple little white eyebrow splotches and a crooked white blaze that runs down the sides of his nose and over his chest, big bat ears. One ear shoots out from his head sideways and the other one points upright but flops at the tip. A fucking mutt.

What kind of photo would that make? Me begging this lame dog to be my friend?

I'm all, dude, they left you here, I may be your only chance. I start to follow him down the street, and he speeds up a little. I pause, and he slows down again. I pick up my speed, but then he does again, too. His legs are long and skinny, speckled with white; he makes galloping away from me look so easy. He should be starving. He looks back over his shoulder at me once, kind of shakes his head so his ears flap, picks up his pace until he starts to soften and blur in the haze hanging at the end of the street. Fuck you, then, I yell at him, and yelling that hard makes me cough so much I puke up a bit of brown and black and white Oreo-rum mess onto the street.

I turn my back on that fucking dog the way he'd turned his back on me, and I walk back to the house. I have to admit, I look back at that dog three or four times, but he just keeps heading as far away from me as he can go, slowly fading into a ghost of a dog, not looking back once, or not that I can see.

Uterus/Uterthem

Day Three — Erica

We form a phalanx around Erica as we exit the clinic. Under her mask, her skin is glazed with perspiration, but she waves at the chanting crowd as if she's the rodeo queen on fair day. The protestors clump and straggle along the length of the green space across the street, five careful bus lengths away from us; there are dozens more protestors than on Day One. They are dappled by the light that threads through the softening fingerbones of newly budding trees: more men than women, a handful of children, a multitude of clashing signs.

Their monotonous chanting scrabbled for traction when they saw us stroll into the clinic for the third day in a row with a different woman at our core. As Erica waves, and we swirl our signs like baton twirlers on parade, their voices rise to howls of rage. They call Erica a murderer, call us evil cunts, spawn of Satan — age-old taunts everyone with a vagina has heard a thousand times. Except, this spawn of Satan isn't flinching.

A cool wind rustles the boulevard trees on this late-spring morning, but as we pulled on our nursery rhyme character masks earlier, in the parking lot — a strategic five winding alleys away from the clinic — we shucked off our jackets, the better to let the protesters see our stomachs. When Michelle removed her flannel overshirt and tossed it in the van, we cheered — none of us are pregnant enough to be showing yet, and so Michelle has added a stomach pad to her costume.

Two days ago, we wouldn't have taunted the crowd like this. We began this project in fear and rage. But as we walked the gauntlet on Day One for Asia's abortion, the protestors' shouts — their clashing signs screaming for the sanctity of life, and for our death — became a discordant, soaring music that lifted our feet, lifted our voices. The fear slid from our skin like pearls of water from an oiled duck, and the rage coalesced into a collective strumming that had us panting with fierce joy. We lifted our feet and planted them firmly on the cracked pavement, revelling in the clumping sound of power.

Michelle steps out of formation to swagger closer to the edge of the fifty-metre safe zone. The crowd noise swirls, punching out individual words among the mass babble: killer, evil, bitch. Sparrows explode from low trees at the outburst, take shelter down the block in calmer pines.

Michelle eyes the protestors, runs her hand lovingly over the thin pink "Baby on Board" T-shirt stretched taut over her rounded foam belly. A dust devil stirs in the gutter, last year's brown-grey leaves kicking and twisting around our synchronized feet.

A man steps forward, shaking a *Murderers should die!* sign. He is pulled back by his companions, who have measured off the safe zone with small, precisely spaced wooden posts that flutter alternating pink and blue ribbons. They scuffle briefly, half-heartedly; he turns back, screams, "Murderers should die!"

"Yes, we can read," Michelle calls to him, and he screams again that murderers should die. His voice cracks, and we laugh. Michelle yells, "See you next week," rubs her belly again.

The man is sweaty and soft; no edges except his slitted eyes and his howling mouth filled with little milk-fed teeth. His skin is poreless and tight over cheeks and jowls — his face would pop if we stuck a pin in it. A red exclamation mark tilts precariously off the edge of his sign.

His friends take up his chorus, and we march in time to their chant. We hoist our signs in rhythm with their song, punching skyward with each "Die!"

Their chant disintegrates into chaotic babble. The sweaty man clenches his fists and yells himself hoarse. And yet neither he nor his companions show any surprise, as if the women they threaten regularly at home, at work, and in front of clinics are always accompanied by fourteen pregnant masked women, marching in lockstep and holding signs that say: 'We're Aborting Because We Can,' 'Against Abortion? Have a Vasectomy,' and 'Pregnancy Is Political/Abortion Is Political.'

Our eyes pass over his rage and that of his spittle-spewing friends to note three police cars approaching. Shelagh winces, moves away from Michelle toward the centre. We nudge her with our elbows, whisper solidarity through our plastic Mother Goose grins. We sweep her to the parking lot at a martial pace, file into the vans. We toss our masks — Humpty Dumpty, sheep, Little Bo Peep, and our favourite, Mary Quite Contrary — in the back of the vans and convoy back to the safe house by circuitous routes to take care of Erica.

Day Five — Shelagh

The clinic is closed today. We're regrouping in the safe house, a heated detached garage in a quiet suburb; we've set it up with a refrigerator, an old pine table extended to its full six battered leaves, a faded teal and rose nineties sofa and loveseat set we rescued from someone's basement, and our crafts area — fence planks and scrap plywood, paint, markers, stencils, cardstock, tape, glue guns. Saws, hammers, and drills. We set up almost a year after the election, when it became clear that matters were only getting worse, and we began to plan our protest.

We're drinking herbal tea and running through the checklist for next week when Shelagh says she thought Michelle's stomach padding was unnecessarily cruel. "We don't need to stick the knife in," she says.

We laugh her down, and she subsides, petulant. We exchange significant looks. She's been getting on our nerves, the way she's begun absently caressing her flat, barely-seven-weeks belly — theatricality is innately tied to the subject matter, it seems.

We exult in Shelagh's choice of words, since sticking the knife in is — literally — our goal. One we've worked hard toward; one that took careful coordination, multiple turkey basters, and more than a few sexual dramatizations. But we're all aware she's becoming a weak link.

Day Seven — Shanice

Apple blossoms are beginning their showy bursts from the street trees as we exit the clinic, Shanice at our centre. The thrumming of insects plumps the sweet air, swelling and mingling with the shouting protestors — the sounds of spring in our new normal. The protestors know our pattern now — the woman at the core is today's killer. Every day their outrage ramps up, and every day it buoys us into the clinic. Every day we exit the clinic proclaiming our fierce resistance with voice and sign.

Anti-protestors now line the other side of the block, shouting in support of our cause, echoing our signs with well-designed slogans intended to go viral. They are required to maintain the same fifty metres as the protestors. They sing and chant, their voices arcing into the air above the street to collide in the floral sky with the voices of the protestors facing them. The police are now a permanent presence at the end of the block, watchful blue lines separating us from our supporters and our opposites.

During our months of organizational meetings — when we were waiting to see whose sticks would glow positive and who would be sent home — we argued about whether our signs should be written in all caps, have every word capitalized, or be sentence case, with only the first word capitalized. Someone — Shelagh? — argued for sentence case, but we voted it down — it doesn't pop from a distance. We argued about whether or not to capitalize 'is' — it's a verb, some argued. But it doesn't look right, others said. Eventually we agreed that grammatical accuracy was a must, and so we capitalized 'is' — in order to be taken seriously, we must not abide a single error on our signs. We agreed that textual variety — a well-planned visual cacophony of lettering, font, and colours — is crucial to connecting with our audiences, and to snagging the eye of the cameras.

As we exit the clinic, we scan the sea of signs, clock with newfound efficiency their effect and style. As we pause for that microsecond, the apple-scented air wafts over us. We breathe deeply once, and return our masked faces to our mission, stirring the bright air alongside the bees.

Now-familiar faces among the protestors include the woman who screams passionately for our souls, who cringes every time her smooth-pored husband raises a fist at us. Sometimes she weeps. Yesterday, Asia called to her, "Marlene, you don't have to stay with your abuser."

We argued about that afterward. We were angry that Asia called the woman Marlene — some of us were angry that the woman mightn't know the comment was aimed at her because Asia assigned her a random name; some of us were angry because singling her out might have triggered her husband to beat her after the protest; some of us were angry because there are stereotypes associated with the name Marlene.

We look Marlene over for bruises, but from our distance, it's hard to tell.

Shanice is relieved to be done, tired of the puking. We thank her for her service, remind her that women's bodies are political tools, whether we are giving birth to please society, or using them to make statements, as we are now. It's all in who controls them.

Beyond the bubble zone, in the sun-warmed park, the crowd roars their outrage. They hate us so much. It makes us laugh fiercely, show them our teeth.

Shanice looks straight into the TV camera, says, "These people should be thanking their god I aborted that child. If I'd raised it, I would have taught it to be a devil worshiper."

Shelagh makes a soft sound of distress; we flick her hard glances before turning back to Shanice, who has made it through her statement and two follow-up questions from the reporter without cracking up. "That's all I have for you," Shanice says briskly, "I have to change my pad."

The crowd roars vengeance; robins watch dispassionately from the street gutters; we whisk Shanice away in the warm blue air.

Day Nine — Louise

The crowds around the clinic have swollen to biblical proportions — protestors and anti-protestors, a chaos of signage, babies in sweet bonnets with cutely misspelled placards taped to their strollers. Rumours are circulating that the Man in Power might show up at the edge of the bubble zone. We're ready.

Louise tosses back a second painkiller, swallows it without water, and strides out the doors. The sun glides across our skin in a knowing caress; she hoists her sign: "My Abortion Was YOUR Fault."

The Man in Power arranges himself for the cameras at the edge of the line of blue and pink fluttering ribbons, his base behind him. He is flanked by several ministers — from his caucus and from the clergy, though that line has become blurred almost beyond recognition in the past year. All have been prominently featured in his government commercials, all are dark suited and vaguely glossy. He allows his followers to scream the hatred, while he and his entourage smoothly wipe disgust from their faces for the benefit of the reporters.

His words are drowned by our singing as we march to face him, far enough away to avoid saliva from his followers, close enough that TV cameras and the crowd's outstretched cell phones will capture our back and forth. The MIP wears a navy suit, a white shirt, and a blue and yellow striped tie. As the cameras swing to focus on us and our own bank of supporters, our eyes track from the sharp points of his hockey announcer collar to the tips of his gleaming shoes. He sees us register the hoodlum beneath his thin veneer, keeps speaking in an attempt to hold the cameras and microphones as they withdraw from him and swivel toward us and our own backdrop of supporters and signs.

We're glad Shelagh called in sick today. We have come to understand that she is only brave when buoyed up in a crowd of women. Enter a disapproving male authority figure, and her resolve melts like spring thaw in the gutter. We'll deal with Shelagh later; right now, it's showtime.

"Every time you deny an impoverished, marginalized, or abused girl or woman birth control, we will have another abortion," Louise says. Her voice rings clear down the block, a reporter's dream. "Our message is simple: if you want us to stop having abortions, you must stop forcing women to conceive."

She holds up her left wrist, encircled loosely by a large man's watch on a worn black leather strap. The hands are frozen at 6:17, barely discernable through a jagged spiderweb of cracks.

"This is a symbol of the violent abuse I suffered at the hands of a man," she says. "That abuse resulted in a pregnancy, because yet another man spent his career denying rape victims the morning after pill."

A reporter thrusts her microphone at Louise. "Your pregnancy is the result of a rape?"

"Not this one," she says. "This is a political statement to those currently in power that no one controls my body but me."

The MIP shakes his head, incredulous. "These women are purposefully creating life in order to wantonly end it," he says in oratorical tones, repeats so the cameras veering back to him will catch the entire sound bite. His crowd jeers. We caress our stomachs and smile like cats.

"Do you want to know why we do this?" we ask, and the cameras swing back. "For the same reason a dog licks its balls," we say. We laugh and leer at him. "Because we can."

With the cameras off and the din of his raging crowd burying his response, his mask slips; he hisses that we are crazy fucking cunts, low so only we catch it.

We jut our nursery rhyme masked faces toward him, hiss back. "Let us put our hands inside your pants," we say. "It's not your body. It's ours." "Where's your jizz? Give us your jizz. It's ours." "You're public property." "It's ours, it's political, it's for the greater good, you belong to us, give us, pin you down, hold your arms," chant, chant, chant until he backs away and the camera batteries wear out and the protestors and anti-protestors lose their voices and the dusk settles, and the birds tuck themselves deep inside shrubs and we float away, crazy fucking cunts.

Day Eleven — Michelle

We are in the safe house, discussing whether or not to film Winnifred's abortion next week and put it on YouTube. There is concern for the clinic. Before the election, they got bomb threats once or twice a year; after, once a week. Now, they average ten a day.

We huddle over our phones, read headlines aloud. We're being pummelled by every news outlet and social media pundit. Previous supporters are now screaming for our heads — this has gone on too long, they say. It's not funny anymore.

We tell each other we think it's still funny. But we aren't sleeping well, and our laughter is harder around the edges.

Michelle staggers through the door spilling a box of pads. Her face is shredded, furious. "I'm fucking miscarrying," she cries.

We push her into a chair, pour her tea.

"If we go now, we can still treat it as an abortion," she says. She tries to stand, doubles over in pain. She beats her fists against the arms of the chair. "I was so close," she weeps.

We assure her there are other functions she can fill, that her role has been important. We reorganize, bump Winnifred up to today. Rebecca stays behind to care for Michelle until she can make her way home. On our way out, we avoid meeting Michelle's eyes. We don't want to say it, but if she isn't pregnant, she's of no use to us.

Day Eleven — Winnifred/Shelagh

As we drive our circuitous route to the clinic, our mood is sombre. We sing, try to pump up the energy as we always do: "It's my uterus, I'll abort if I want to, abort if I want to, abort if I want to. You would abort too if it happened to you!"

We're groping for the simmering tension that has propelled us this far. But we miss Louise, and Michelle, and Shanice.

We park in our hidden lot, pull out our Mother Goose masks. Crushed apple blossoms stir at our feet and burst their last pockets of scent as we march through the alleys toward the clinic, Winnifred at our centre.

When we see Shelagh fronting the now-silent protestors, we understand that we should be grateful she didn't lead them to the parking lot, that she chose to stage the showdown at the scene of the crime, where the police have some chance of stopping the riot before people are killed. But it's hard to feel grateful as she throws the first overripe tomato. It's odd to hear it splatter wet and solid against one of our neatly painted signs, in a zone usually so filled with shouting. The tomato unleashes a torrent of fruit, stones, a cacophony of rage. Signs become shields, splinter into stakes in our bleeding hands. Birds erupt from the rattling trees and flee the block in dark, incensed swoops.

Marlene's husband throws a Molotov cocktail, and the safe zone lights up.

And the ties of the plastic liquor store bag fan out like wings

Zoë is on the porch, painting her toenails deep purple. The tree to her right shivers in a gust of wind; birds dart among the leaves. A small nuthatch dances up and down the trunk, tapping at the bark. Zoë sticks the brush back in the bottle and grabs her cell phone, zooms in for a burst of pictures of the nuthatch. She hasn't yet managed to capture the rust-red markings on its head in her drawings.

Through the open kitchen window, the smack of wooden cupboard doors opening and closing, the clatter of pots. She stretches her legs and wiggles her feet up and down; the steady breeze might make the first coat dry faster. The refrigerator door opens and closes, the ice-maker rattles into a glass. It's just after 4:30. Her mother will drink this one quickly — her first official drink of the day — then a refill before she looks for her daughter. Zoë has ten minutes, tops. She is adding the final quick strokes to the second coat when the ice-maker clatters again.

"Zoë, come help with dinner."

She twists the cap on the bottle of polish. "Where's Jerome?"

"It doesn't matter. Come in and help."

"It's sexist to make the girl work in the kitchen while the boy sits downstairs playing video games."

Mary's face appears in the window. "Jerome will do the dishes. Get in here. Now."

Her feet slap on the kitchen tiles as she moves toward the door. Zoë rolls her eyes and gets up. She walks bow legged and splay footed to avoid smudging her still-damp toes, lets the screen door slam behind her.

Her mother looks at the nail polish and cell phone in her hands. "You've been busy."

"I only got off work an hour ago. I had to shower to get rid of the pizza smell. All the animals in the neighbourhood were stalking —"

"I called Mr. Raymond about your university applications," Mary says.

Zoë tenses, her breath catching. "You phoned the school counsellor? What time did you call?"

"Sometime before lunch. But he was in a meeting, and I ran out of time to call him back."

Zoë exhales again, relaxes her clenched hands. "You don't need to phone him. I'll get them done. And he's no help anyway."

Mary raises an eyebrow, picks up her glass and drinks. "Peel the shrimp."

Zoë peels shrimp and sets them aside. She fills a pot with water for the pasta, puts it on the back of the stove. Her mother crushes garlic and selects the spices she wants, arranging them by colour along the countertop. She pulls out the cutting board and palms tomatoes and onions from a yellow bowl by the window. She takes a knife from the block, saws at the overripe tomato; it squirts seeds, bounces out of her hand. Zoë steps forward, takes the knife from her mother. "Let me."

Mary splashes more vodka and soda into her glass, the ice still plentiful from her last top-up. She leans against the counter and sips her drink. "How was work?"

"Lousy. Monica called in sick, and the cook is a jerk. Today he —"

"You think everyone's a jerk."

The cook had pressed himself against Zoë three times today as she was loading dirty plates into the industrial dishwasher. He is almost her father's age, but short and hairy. He smells like pepperoni. The delivery guy saw him do it; he's a year older than

Zoë, and they speak as seldom as possible. When he saw the cook rub himself against Zoë, and saw her jerk away in disgust, he smirked and walked out the back door, his arms piled high with pizza boxes. Zoë spent her shift avoiding the kitchen as much as possible.

"You're right, I'm the jerk."

Her father comes in and Zoë squeals, "Daddy!" She runs to him and hugs him, not letting go until her mother slaps her glass down on the counter, irritation sharpening her voice.

"Will you please remind your daughter that she needs to fill out these university applications?"

George slings his briefcase onto the kitchen counter. "Come on, Zoë, focus. How are you going to succeed if you don't get your applications done? You've got the talent, but where's your drive?"

George is the coordinator for the provincial coaching association, and this is how he talks.

Zoë grits her teeth and abandons the pretense that he's her favourite. "I don't know what I want to take."

Mary sighs, swirls the ice in her almost empty glass. Her frown smooths out slowly, the pieces of her face shifting like a smeary jigsaw puzzle. "You aren't picking classes yet. You just have to have a focus. Like education, or business."

"Or recreation," says George. "There are dozens of ways you can go with a recreation degree."

"What if I want to take art?"

Mary tosses the spoon she's been stirring with onto the counter, spattering tomato bits on the grey speckled countertop. "George, talk to her. If you want to do art, then do art education. At least you'll have a job. We're not putting out all this money so you can waste yourself at some part-time shit job typing other people's memos."

"Your mom's right," George says. He picks up the spoon and sets it in the spoon rest on the stove. He turns down the heat under the sauce and wipes the counter. "The practical choice is to combine it with teaching. You can do your art in your spare time."

"So, you agree with Mom that she has a shit job?"

Mary frowns, and George puts his arm around her, kisses her cheek. "Dinner smells great, honey."

Mary smiles up at him. "Thanks. Want a drink?"

"Sure, why not?"

Zoë walks to the basement stairs and smacks the railing hard, rattling the wood against the metal brackets. "Jerome, dinner's almost ready."

He doesn't answer, and she walks down the stairs, rubbing her stinging hand. Jerome is lounging on the couch flipping between late hockey and early baseball games. He graduated last year with the pizza delivery guy. Now he's taking classes through the city's satellite campus, working to bring up his science grades. He and his parents have high hopes of a sports scholarship. All the available paperwork has long been completed.

"Come save me from these lunatics," she says.

Jerome yawns and tosses the remote onto the table. "God, Zoë, you need to take a pill. You're always crying about something."

"Maybe I have reason to cry. No one cares that some horny guy old enough to be my father is playing ass-grab with me at work. This whole fucking family is allergic to reality."

Jerome pushes himself off the couch. "Did you tell Dad?"

"That the family's allergic to reality?"

"About the horny old guy."

"I tried last week, but you know how he makes excuses for people who act like assholes. He interrupted me fast, before I could say anything that might make him uncomfortable, and said it was probably all a misunderstanding. He told me to open up a dialogue."

"Do you want me to kick this guy's ass?"

Zoë snorts. "You'd get arrested, and I'd get fired, and it would be all my fault that you didn't get your precious sports scholarship."

Jerome shrugs. "Then quit."

She stomps back upstairs. Jerome leaves the TV on, and the soft drone of sports announcers trails behind them into the dining room.

George sets the silverware on the table and steers Mary to her chair. "You sit. You've done enough."

Mary plays with a fresh drink as George carries in the pasta bowl; she leans forward to ladle it onto their plates. A basket of white paper napkins sits in the centre of the table, and George uses one to wipe splashes of pasta sauce from the gleaming wood. He takes it into the kitchen and slides back into his chair.

Jerome digs in. "Smells great, Mom. Thanks."

Zoë rolls her eyes.

George sips his beer; Mary sips her drink and reminisces about a former teacher. Mrs. Miller had once read a poem Mary wrote aloud to the class, as an example of good metre. "I always wanted to be a teacher," Mary says. "Helping to form the minds of tomorrow."

George pats her hand and says any student would have been lucky to have her as their teacher. He keeps his eyes focused on Mary while Zoë stares at him. Jerome shovels in his pasta, surreptitiously checking his phone under the table.

"I've never forgotten her. She had such an impact on me." Mary's words are thick, as if her tongue has swollen. Her hands move to her mouth and back to the table in an unsteady but methodical rhythm, a forkful of food, a sip from the glass, another forkful, another sip. "Zoë, don't you want to make a difference like that?"

Zoë blinks, stares down at her plate. Such a cheery buttercup pattern, tracing the outside of the plate with tiny bits of gold leaf, smeared now at the edges with drying tomato chunks and herbs, a partial shrimp tail she'd missed. She nods. Her throat is too tight; she couldn't speak if she tried. The food is sitting right there, right at the back of her throat, tapping at her, threatening to pour back out in chunky waves of fettucine and shrimp. She tenses her body to hold it all back, starts counting silently even as she meets her mother's fuzzy gaze and nods again. Mary and George rhapsodize about the rewards of teaching and coaching and mentoring. Zoë pushes a limp noodle around on her plate, making a rough scallop pattern of the red stains.

Jerome shoves back his chair. "Gotta go. Coach said we had to be there early tonight."

Zoë's chair wobbles as she jumps to her feet, and she reaches back to steady it. She walks around the table stacking plates. "Guess that leaves me with the dishes."

Mary hands Zoë her plate. "Thanks, dear."

When she's finished, Zoë escapes to her room. She opens her window. The day's wind has subsided into a soft spring evening; she gulps in the scent of lilacs and sits on her bed. She flips through her sketch book, frowning at the unnatural angle of the arms on the girl she's been drawing — a pierced, sullen stranger Zoë often sees on the bus. The girl doesn't make eye contact with anyone, but not in a shy way — more as if she simply doesn't waste time on irrelevant people. Her hair is impossibly black, a dull matte that seems to suck up the light rather than reflecting anything back. Zoë has drawn a close-up of the girl's ear, hair falling over multiple piercings. But her eyeliner is all wrong: strong and thick, yet not managing to scream fuck off — it doesn't even whisper fuck off, really.

The bird drawings are better, at least the ones when they aren't in flight. Some of the sketches of elongated wings secretly please Zoë, the details on the feathers.

She's only kept one drawing of the boy she knew who was killed last year, tiny, jagged shreds of paper at the top of the sketch book the only remaining evidence of other drawings of him that she'd ripped out. In this one, the boy has branches in his hair, burning eyes; he is lying in unmown grass. Zoë pauses at it then flips to a clean page. She thumbs through the nuthatch photos on her phone and zooms in on one. The wings are too blurred for detail but the colour is good. She picks up a soft grey pencil, sketches its long, skinny beak in a few strokes. Her parents' voices are a faint murmur downstairs, her mother's rising then falling again, her father's low and soothing.

Sunday after supper Zoë is sitting on the porch again, texting Monica. *Please be at work Thursday. Creepy Andy keeps grabbing me.* The wind swings the bird feeder on its low branch, rattles the maple leaves. The days are getting longer, the sun high and sparkling through the waving trees.

A single piercing chirp cuts through the background bird sounds. Then again. Not the normal call of a sparrow: this sounds urgent, demanding.

Not a chickadee, either, or the one-note peep of a nuthatch. Zoë has learned to recognize the most familiar bird calls from sitting on the porch watching them for so many hours, trying to draw them. When she was younger, in a different life altogether, Mary would sit beside her and point out the various species.

Zoë's cell phone vibrates, and Monica's response appears on the screen. *Blowing off work 4 Arsenic Machine concert. Sorry!! Kick him in the nuts.*

Zoë mutters curses and shoves her cell back in her pocket.

The chirp comes again. Insistent. Closer than before. She looks down the length of the porch and finally sees it. A brown sparrow, sitting motionless at the far end, watching her. She walks toward it slowly, surprised when it remains in place. It chirps again. It is sleekly plump, brown feathers ruffling in the light breeze.

She takes another step, reaches out a finger; it still doesn't move. She bends, strokes the small brown head. The sparrow doesn't flinch. Its eyes look sleepy, content. She strokes it again. She thinks of bird lice, but can't resist. It's amazing to be allowed to touch this small wild bird. She crouches beside it. "Don't be afraid," she says. The sparrow watches her. She touches it again, runs her finger down its soft back. It must be hurt. There's no way it would sit here like this otherwise.

A crow calls from a tree two houses down, another answers. There are crows all over this neighbourhood. And cats. Her mother is constantly complaining about cat shit in the flowerbeds. Zoë looks around the yard, then straightens and walks back to the house, looking over her shoulder at the bird. In the entryway, she takes a box her mother has flattened for recycling, pushes it back into shape. Her parents are sitting at the table looking through university calendars. Mary has a highball glass beside her; George has a beer. Zoë can hear Jerome's television from the basement. She takes an old towel from the cupboard beneath the sink, still not sure what she'll do.

The sparrow is where she left it, blinking in the sunlight. She approaches again, the towel draped loosely around one hand, box in the other. She tries to pick up the sparrow using her towelled hand, but she's awkward, afraid of hurting it. The sparrow dodges her and tries to take flight. It makes a clumsy circle a foot in the air before falling back to the deck.

"It's okay," she says. "I want to help you." This time, she gets her hand around the bird. Through the towel, its tiny heart pulses against her fingers. She sets it gently in the box. It flaps its wings twice, but she can't tell if either one is broken.

She goes into the house, takes a small saucer from the china cabinet, sprays water into it from the hose attached to the side of the house. Maybe the sparrow will be gone by the time she returns. Maybe it hit the window and is only stunned. But when she returns, it's still sitting in the box. It hasn't chirped since she first touched it. She sets the saucer of water in the box and turns to the plastic tub of bird seed her mother keeps on the deck. The wood planks around it are strewn with spilled seed, and warnings from an earlier version of Mary linger in her mind — spilled seed attracts mice, spreads weeds. Zoë scrapes up the fallen seed with her hands, deposits it next to the saucer.

She turns toward the house, then back to the box. She closes two of the flaps and lays the towel across them to hold them down. There is a gap, enough to allow air in, but now the bird is safe from Tiger Lily next door, or the white cat that likes to sleep in their flowerbed.

Mary looks up when Zoë enters, her face dreamy. "What are you doing out there? Have a look at these course lists. I'd kill to take some of these classes."

"There's a wounded bird on our deck. I didn't know what to do with him, so I put him in a box." She moves to the sink and turns on the tap, lathering her hands with antibacterial soap.

Mary pushes back her chair. "You handled a sick bird? It probably has West Nile."

"Your mother's right. Birds carry disease," George says. "You have to be careful."

"I used a towel to pick him up, and I'm washing my hands," Zoë says. "What did you want me to do? Leave him out there so the neighbours' cats could shred him on our porch?"

"Of course not." Mary frowns and drains her drink.

"Come look at him." Zoë leads her parents outside. The sparrow blinks but doesn't move as she opens the box flaps again to allow them to peer in.

"It does look healthy," George says. "It's very fat."

"Just don't bring it in the house," Mary says, eyeing the box with distaste.

"I'm trying to do the right thing."

"If you're worried about doing something right, maybe you could fill out those application forms," Mary says. "I feel sorry for the bird, but school is more important."

"You're the one who brings them here with all the birdseed you put out. Doesn't that mean you have responsibility for them?"

Mary's face shifts. When she looks into Zoë's eyes, her own are moist, fuzzily affectionate. "I feed birds. I have responsibility for you."

"He was looking right at me and chirping," Zoë says. Her voice comes out small and thin. "I didn't know what to do, but I couldn't leave him to die on our deck."

"It will be fine," George says. "Just let it sort itself out." Her parents go back inside the house. A moment later, the ice maker rattles.

The sparrow hasn't moved since Zoë put it in the box. She closes the flaps and replaces the towel over them. She sits on the step, lifts her face to the sun.

When she goes back inside, her parents are sitting at the table again. The university calendars and application forms are piled in front of Zoë's chair.

"Come look through these calendars with us, get some excitement going," George says.

Zoë takes the stack from the table. "I'll look at them on my own. I can't handle the pressure from you two."

"Honey, it's not pressure," George says. "It's encouragement."

Before bed she goes outside to check on the sparrow. She's relieved to hear flapping from the box — the bird must be recovered, and indignant at being held captive. But when she removes the towel and lifts the flaps, he is hunched over on himself, one wing dragging in the edge of the water saucer. His weight is resting on his head. A brief rustle of wings again; the head stays down.

Her stomach drops. She slaps the flaps closed and puts the towel back in place. In the house, she washes her hands under too-hot water.

Her father calls from the living room, "How is it?"

Zoë looks in. "Where's Mom?"

"Your mother's tired today. She went to bed early."

Zoë stares at her father for a long moment, then drops her eyes. "I think it's dying."

She walks up the stairs, unable to shake the image of it — of how the bird had collapsed on itself. She gags as she brushes her teeth.

In her room, she pulls a university calendar from the stack on her dresser, flips to the Fine Arts section. The course descriptions and prerequisites sound glamorous and remote. She takes her portfolio from the closet and flips through it. She had amassed a few pieces she'd been proud of during her art class last semester. Now she sees flaws everywhere.

The next morning, Zoë follows Mary to the door as she leaves for work, gestures at the box on the porch. "You were right. It's not wounded. It's sick."

"We'll get your dad to take care of it when he gets home."

"I thought I was protecting it from the cats, but now I think I should have left it," Zoë says. "I'm just prolonging its pain."

"Give yourself a break," Mary says. "You're only seventeen. How would you know what needs protecting and what should be left alone?" There are faint blue shadows under her eyes, beneath her careful make-up.

"Mom —"

Mary walks past the box and gets into the car. She honks as she pulls out of the driveway.

The bird's wings are tucked up against its body. Its head is still down in that unnatural position. A small pool of shit has spread under its tail.

Zoë wraps the towel around her hand. The fabric makes her clumsy as she picks up the bird; she turns it over. She can't tell if it's dead or not. Its eyes are clouded over, or are they closed?

The sparrow flutters wildly in her hand. It startles Zoë, and her hand jerks open. The bird falls to the deck, landing on its back. Its wings rattle and subside. She tightens the towel around her hand and reaches for the bird. Its feet clutch at her fingers through the fabric; when she lifts her hand, it hangs upside down from it. She wraps the towel around the bird and turns it right-side up, surprised and repelled at the strength of its tiny claws. She tries to put it back in the box, but it won't release her fingers. She has to shake it loose from the towel; she has to shake it three times before it falls into the box on its back. She nudges it right-side up with the towel; it subsides into a heap, weight once again resting on its head. Zoë closes the box and walks back into the house. She washes her hands until the water is too hot to bear.

The sullen girl isn't on the bus. Zoë sways with the rhythm of stops and starts, its wide sweeps around the corners. The sullen girl wouldn't be obsessing about a dying bird. She'd kick disgusting Andy in the nuts. As for a mother who's a drunk and a father and brother who pretend she's not? The black-haired girl would tell them all to fuck off. Maybe that's the only way to get adults to listen.

She thinks of the sparrow as she moves through her classes, of its warm brown body, at first so plump and vibrant under her fingers. She thinks of its insistent call to her, the way it later collapsed, leaning on its head. The pool of white and grey under its tail. She scrubs her hands several times throughout the day. That afternoon she goes to a meeting about graduation, listens to talk about dresses, the prom, university. The prom colours are pink and grey; there will be a large balloon arch in these colours, and three smaller ones.

When she gets home, Zoë passes the box on the porch, goes into the house, and tosses her backpack on the kitchen floor. She pours herself a glass of water, drinks it standing at the sink. Finally, she steps back outside.

The trees in the yard are filled with chickadees, sparrows, and jays vying for branch space around the feeder. A pair of nuthatches lurk on the next tree, unwilling to join the fray. Zoë watches them, scratches her fingers hard, as if the sparrow's insistent claws are still clinging to her through the towel.

She opens the box and peers in. The pool of shit has become larger, laced with yellow, black and white. The sparrow is still lying with its weight on its head, its brown back moving up and down.

She picks up the box and walks down the porch steps, around the house through the side gate and into the back yard.

She sets the box on the raised wooden flowerbed at the east side of the yard. The last few petals on her mother's tulips droop and flutter into the dirt, their stalks browning. The snowdrop anemones have gone to seed, their heads thin with the last remnants of fluff that haven't yet been taken by the wind.

She digs out her key and unlocks the back door, goes upstairs to her room. She brings down the pile of calendars, the admission forms and a pen. She stacks the forms on the kitchen table.

She searches through the pantry for plastic bags. The ones from the grocery store all have small holes in the bottom. She finds two solid bags from her mother's favourite liquor store. She checks her phone; her mother will be home soon. She leaves her phone on the table, carries the bags out the back door and down to the flowerbed.

Zoë leans over the box. The sparrow's back is still moving up and down. It hasn't changed position. She puts the liquor store bag on her hand and lifts the sparrow out, careful to grip it firmly so its claws can't clutch at anything. She flips the bag inside out around the little brown bird, knots and double knots the bag. The sparrow's wings flutter and the plastic bag rustles. She slips it inside the second plastic bag, double knots that one, too.

Zoë sits on the edge of the flowerbed, face to the sun. A gust of wind rattles the bag, and the tied ends fan out for a moment, like wings. She watches it for a while before moving her gaze back to the trees, the blue sky. Crows call out behind her.

A car door slams, then the front door as her mother enters the house. The plastic bag rustles again. Mary calls her name, quietly at first and then louder and more insistently. Finally, she stops calling. Ice rattles against glass. Zoë waits, staring at the thrashing trees.

An old lady and her hair

There are two people you hate in the world — a pastor and a hairstylist named Jennifer. You've heard the pastor, once, orating from his pulpit, and that was plenty; you never plan on meeting Jennifer.

At Abilene's funeral, Pastor Plage said, "Abilene was a special person, with special gifts." You sat in a pew in the middle of the near-empty church, clutching Matthew's hand. The minister paused, and you waited for him to list some of her special gifts, maybe even talk about her unusual hair, but that was all he had to say about Abilene before going on to talk about God and eternal rest and the comfort of the scriptures. Twenty-plus years Abilene had been a member of his congregation — she'd been to his home for lunch, for Christ's sake, those annual mercy lunches with the other widows — and he couldn't come up with a single story about Abilene's special gifts. Plage's voice was carefully sonorous, like he thought the deep, grave sounds he made replaced substance.

When Matthew's modelling took off and he quit hairdressing, he trained you on the intricacies of setting Abilene's hair. Abilene was always early for her appointment, waiting in her block-long Chrysler every Saturday morning when you pulled into the parking lot. She tottered in behind you on thin high heels. You kept waiting for her to snap an ankle. While you put the coffee on and counted the float and the rest of the staff straggled in,

Abilene sat on the bench, folding last night's clean towels into horizontal quarters, the way stylists like them.

"Just ignore me," she'd say, but as soon as you said anything, she'd start to talk. You'd compliment her skirt, and she'd be off on a story about how she used to beat her brothers at baseball, even wearing her unwieldy skirts. Because farm girls didn't wear pants. You'd nod, make occasional noises to show you were listening. Then you'd lose track of the float and have to start counting all over again.

One Saturday morning, Abilene didn't come. You counted the cash without error while the jumbled basket of towels sat on the bench. You dialed Abilene's number.

"Oh, Susan, I was just about to call you. Lisa and Barry are visiting from Edmonton." Her voice was pleased. "It's Susan, my hair stylist," she said to someone in the background. "I'm afraid I worried her."

"Ah, the famous Lisa," you said. "Tell her I said hi."

Abilene brought it up a few times. "I felt so badly for worrying you." The first time she said it, you laughed and brushed it off, told her it was nothing. The second time, you fumbled it, understood too late. The third time, you put your hand on her shoulder and said, "You did, you worried me."

One Saturday, you arrived at work with bleared red eyes and an extra coat of mascara to compensate. The night before, you'd had a heartbreaking, grovelling fight with an elusive boy who loved how much you loved him — almost as much as he loved how great it felt to brush against your fingers before gliding through them. He was calm. You were anything but. You think he laughed. You definitely remember him saying that you took things too seriously. It took mortifying minutes to shove your feet into your soft knee-high boots; they kept flopping over, and you had to stop twice to wipe your face with the hem of the satiny red tank top you would never feel pretty in again but kept for two more years because you were poor and didn't want to throw away a perfectly good shirt. You cried leaving his house, cried even more when he didn't stop you. You stumbled eleven blocks home in a chill wind.

Your head pounded in time with your fingers as you shampooed Abilene's hair. The benches at the front of the salon were full — five kids between the ages of two and seven, a teenage boy with a heavily razored punk cut, a highlighted blonde woman with a graduated bob. After Abilene, you didn't have any regular clients booked until noon. That meant you'd have to deal with these walk-ins, and that meant almost certainly chopping open at least one knuckle over the head of a squirming kid, even if you were lucky enough to avoid the punk. You saw your future, and it included the search for bandages while some hovering mother grimaced at the thought of your blood in her twitchy angel's hair.

You sank into the chair next to Abilene's, flicked bubbles from your fingers onto its black fake leather arm. "I know you aren't due for a perm for another two weeks, but can we do it today, instead?"

Your voice caught; when she agreed, you had to blink fast to clear your vision. Abilene was still lying back in the sink, hair sculpted into swirls of rich coconut-scented shampoo. She couldn't see your face. But she patted your hand.

And so you sectioned her and wrapped her up in neatly aligned pink rods. And you talked as you worked. You didn't tell Abilene that you'd slapped at Dion's chest, or that his reaction was to laugh, and you didn't tell her how drunk you'd been, but you did give her an edited version over the next few hours. Your voice was low so the other stylists and clients wouldn't hear; your hands grew steadier as you worked, the tension as perfect on every perm rod as any well-strung violin.

"I know what you mean," Abilene said. "Leland used to drive me so crazy, I could have cheerfully strangled him a few times."

You laughed at the thought. Leland died before you started doing Abilene's hair, back when she was Matthew's customer, and your only contact was to roll your eyes every Saturday morning as you stumbled past Abilene's cheerful greetings on your way to your station to plug in your curling irons. But you paused your comb and scissors to call hello when Leland picked Abilene up after her appointments. All the stylists did.

Leland was an old-school gentleman. He wore bow ties: red, floral yellow, striped navy blue. You danced the polka with him at Matthew and Jeromy's wedding; his hand was light on your back, steering you around the floor. That night his bow tie was purple, to match the wedding colours.

"He treated me like a child," Abilene said. "It seemed sweet at first, but he was always protecting me." You took Abilene to the staff room, a plastic bag on her head while her perm processed. You bummed one of her menthol cigarettes. An old, irresistible habit — leaning in, extending the swaying flame from a green plastic lighter toward the waiting white tip, breathing out together in a cloud of grey satisfaction.

"When he died, I wanted to kill him myself. I had no idea how to pay the bills or take care of the banking." Abilene blew smoke away from you and to the side; she tapped her cigarette against the ceramic ashtray in a three-beat gesture you'd come to recognize. Her wedding and anniversary rings were polished so the small diamond chips glinted. Her nails were matte coral. "Imagine," she said, "At age seventy, trying to learn what every woman should have known all along."

You twirled your ashes against the side of the ashtray. "You looked like such a charming couple. I never thought about the downside of chivalry."

"Oh, he was good to me," Abilene said. "But he thought he was smarter than me, and he wasn't. If I had to do it again, I'd set out a few rules right from the start."

The perm was to give Abilene's fine hair more body, make her set last. She wouldn't have been caught dead in a wash and wear, even before perms went out of fashion. Every Saturday morning, you eased out a week's worth of backcombing and product at the sink, running your fingers through the knots again and again, feeling the build-up of hairspray soften and release beneath the warm spray and the thick coconut-scented lather. You wrapped her head smartly in one of the towels she'd folded, guided her from the sink to your chair. You'd work in a leave-in conditioner — for protection from all the heat you were about to apply, and to add bulk. Next, a rich, creamy mousse for control without added weight. When you blow-dried her hair, you worked the roots to add height.

At this point, Abilene looked like a dandelion gone to seed, a normal foundational part of the process that neither of you remarked on. Once her hair was dry, you lightly stroked a styling cream through it, licking your finger to test the heat of your curling iron. It was a small barrel iron, the size of white perm rods. You took small sections — the size of the barrel width, no bigger — and curled them upward from Abilene's neck and ears until they met at the top of her head. You sprayed each section with a light sculpting spray as you worked your way around Abilene; the fine mist sizzled on the barrel. The curls were crisp and tight, they shone with product. Then you backcombed the living hell out of it until it was a huge, frizzy mess — twice the original dandelion.

This is where the shaping began, atop the solid base of backcombing you'd created. You combed the surface of the sides and back, straight up; delicately so you wouldn't disturb the matted hair underneath. Then you used your hand, smoothing the surface in careful, repetitive motions, as if you were stroking a cat, or a cranky baby. You sprayed the sides and back flat, ran your hand over it, followed by your blow dryer to create a smooth, solid surface that could be slept on for a week. This sleek, plastic surface culminated in high, arranged curls at the top. You pinched at the curls, defining them as you sprayed. The process took an hour, you circling Abilene like a planet. The set got more extreme over the years, higher at the top and flatter at the sides.

158

You met Brent, and Dion's beer-fuelled laughter faded from your mind faster than you'd thought possible. Brent worked in a print shop and played bass in a weekend band when they could scrape together a gig. And then you were making plans to go away for the weekend. You trained your replacement the Saturday before you left, calling her over to observe each step of your work on Abilene, demonstrating the proper way to backcomb. Marie didn't seem to take her substitute role seriously; she kept looking at the waiting clients, anxious to build her hourly commission. You came back from the mountains exhausted, with fading brown marks on your upper arms that made you smile every morning when you covered them with careful sleeves. Abilene's set hadn't lasted three days.

"I will never trust you to her again," you said. "Your hair reflects on me, too."

She met your eyes in the mirror. "She's still a virgin," she whispered. "She's never even kissed a boy."

You lowered your curling iron and stared at her reflection. "Why on earth would she tell you that?"

"She thought I'd be impressed," Abilene said. "But it's ridiculous. How will a girl know she's met the right man if she's never kissed anyone else?"

"And by kissed, you mean . . ."

She clapped her hands like a five-year-old and laughed, which made you laugh harder. With that, you were firmly into the realm of topics stylists were instructed never to discuss with clients. "Don't tell Pastor Plage, but I agree with abortion," Abilene said. "It's absolutely necessary sometimes." She put her hand over her mouth as if she were saying something naughty, then she removed it again and you leaned over and kissed her powdered cheek.

These were a few of the special gifts Pastor Plage didn't detail at Abilene's funeral. People saw a tiny old woman with a home manicure and old-fashioned, perfect pantyhose, wobbling along on high heels; they'd think they knew her. And they'd be wrong.

The axis shifted that Christmas. Abilene normally took the Greyhound to Lisa and Barry's house, but this year they were travelling to Montreal to spend the holidays with their oldest son instead. It would be Abilene's first Christmas alone, and your first Christmas wishing you weren't.

You drove the dark, straight highway to your mother's silent house on Christmas Eve, while Brent drove across the city to his mother's. You arrived late and were woken at eight am; you called Brent and mumbled sleepy greetings. And then you thought of Abilene; she would have been up for hours by then; she wasn't much of a sleeper. She would have taken her time getting ready for church, touching up her nails. She would be wearing her pink wool jacket and matching skirt, with the brown strappy shoes. After you'd exchanged small stacks of neatly wrapped presents with your mother, worked for an hour on the annual puzzle, you picked up the phone again.

"Are you wearing your pink outfit?"

"You know me so well," she said. "Pastor Plage had a few ladies over for lunch. It's been a lovely day."

When you got home you dumped your bags and rushed to Brent's apartment. "I don't want to spend Christmas without you next year," you said. You looked at his tabletop tree, made from beer cans. "But could we put up a real tree?"

He laughed. "Typical woman, trying to change me."

When you got engaged, you took Brent to Abilene's apartment for tea. She opened the door wearing mules, with thin heels and pink marabou on the toes. She set out shortbread cookies on a flowered plate, tea in dainty china cups with gold leaf on the curving, slight handles. She gave you a bottle of Piesporter Michelsberg in a flowered gift bag. You removed the silver ribbons that she'd curled into cascading ringlets and tied around the neck of the bottle, put them in your purse.

Before you left, Brent offered to change a hard-to-reach light bulb.

"I don't want to be a bother," Abilene said. "The landlord comes on Thursday."

"We can't have you wandering around in the dark," Brent said.

She smiled up at him and led him to the closet where she kept her stepstool. To you she said, "This boy is a keeper."

As you walked to the door, Brent wrote his cell phone number on a print shop business card, stuck it to Abilene's refrigerator with a magnet of yellow poppies. "I don't want you getting up on that stool for any reason," he said. "Call me any time."

Brent was smiling as you drove away.

You took his hand. "You're a good man," you said.

"It was such a simple thing to do. She made it sound like I was a hero."

"You are," you said. He looked surprised. This was not the way you spoke to each other.

Prices went up every year at the salon, but you never got around to telling Abilene. By the end of your hairdressing career, you were practically working on her for free. It seemed a small forgiveness at the time.

One sunny Saturday, Abilene turned her face to the open salon window and breathed in the lilacs that suffused the room from the hedge bordering the parking lot. Top 40 music played in the background. "Susan, promise me you'll do my hair for my funeral."

You removed your curling iron from a shining silver sausage curl, lowered your comb. "Don't talk like that. You're going to be around for a long time."

Abilene waved her hand dismissively. Her rings glinted in the sunlight falling across your chair. "Please, Susan, tell me you'll do it. I want to look my best."

You paused, then nodded. "And you'll wear your pink suit?"

"Yes. I know it's your favourite."

When you and Brent got married, Abilene was in an aisle seat, touching your outstretched hand as you walked past on your mother's stiff arm. She waltzed with Brent, your cousin, and the lead singer of Brent's band. She kissed you. "You are so beautiful," she said. "Don't make the same mistake I did — set the rules early on."

Her hair had been set by one of the other girls at the salon that morning, a careful comb-out too similar to all the grandmothers in the room. She wore the pink suit.

And the following Christmas marked the next cycle in your little evolution. Your silent mother met a widower, and, in a fashion utterly unrecognizable to you, flew away with him to a seniors' beach resort in Maui for the holidays. Abilene stopped travelling. And your new mother-in-law — as different a widow from your mother as you could imagine — loved a crowded dinner table.

Abilene arrived forty-five minutes before dinner and stayed an hour afterward. She was a chatterbox in your chair, but in mixed company, she was the ideal dinner guest: everyone at the table expanded easily, naturally, under Abilene's approving gaze. Your mother-in-law told stories you hadn't heard about her childhood in corn country; that's also how you learned that Abilene's ringed, carefully painted hands had helped birth animals, had practised composting decades before it was fashionable. Abilene didn't switch hands after cutting her meat; she raised it to her mouth with her left hand. At the end of the meal, she placed her fork neatly beside her knife, tines down.

It was Brent's job to pick up Abilene each year and drive her home again after supper. Even during the last, miserable Christmas of your marriage, he did this willingly. She walked into the house on his arm, and he dusted the snow from her coat before hanging it in the closet; he pulled out her chair at the table.

Abilene smiled up at him. "You know how to make an old lady feel special."

Sometimes, when you feel angry about the random cruelties you and Brent slipped into the habit of piling on each other, you remember this: when he took Abilene's coat from the closet after supper and helped her into it, when you moved in for her embrace, your eyes met Brent's, and you smiled at each other over Abilene's head in a brief moment of shared affection.

You stopped emailing your mother-in-law a year after the divorce, but you miss her most, now, when you think of her standing at the door at Christmas, exclaiming over the poinsettia in Abilene's hands, saying, "Abilene, I've been looking forward to seeing you all year."

In what you would later recognize as the final year of hopefulness in your marriage, you and Brent moved to another city; he managed a print shop in the same chain and found another weekend band. You moved from doing hair to repping one of the haircare lines your salon had carried. You travelled the province, sometimes with the sleek-haired man who used to sell you the same products, adapting his charming sales pitches for your own use. Eventually your lower back stopped seizing every morning.

When you were back in your former city, you and Abilene would have lunch at La Trattoria, surrounded by plants and shrubs strung with fairy lights and soft music. You ordered Caesars with your salads. You'd scrutinize Abilene's set. It was never high enough on top or smooth enough on the sides and back. You'd stand by the decorative shrubs outside afterward, sneak guilty glances around the parking lot as you dragged on one of her menthols.

"Tell Jennifer she needs to backcomb with the wide end of a wave comb, not with a pick," you'd say. "Tell her to use her blow dryer on the sides."

"That's why you need to do it for my funeral," Abilene said.

"I promise."

That final Christmas, Abilene wore your least favourite of her blouses — cream polyester with a big, floppy bow at the neck — a straight brown skirt, and her usual heels. Her hair still wasn't high enough on top, though the sides were flatter. She'd taken to sleeping on a satin pillowcase to hold the set better.

When Brent made a joke at your expense, Abilene didn't laugh. She turned to smile at you before looking around the table. "I appreciate your goodness," she said. "You're all so very kind to include me in your family dinner."

"You are my family," you said. You looked at your plate, focused on plugging a hole in the wall of potatoes you'd created so your gravy wouldn't leak onto your carrots.

After dinner, Caesars in hand, you took Abilene onto the covered back deck; it was a mild winter. You sat side by side in near silence, smoking.

Abilene squeezed your hand. Her fingernails were the same matte coral they'd been since the day you met. You looked down at your hands; you could still see grace and girlishness in Abilene's fingers.

Matthew called a few months later. You were sitting at the dining room table with Brent, mired in a dull, hostile silence. When the phone rang, you leapt for it. Abilene was dead. Lisa had called the salon, unable to remember your married name. Word got to Matthew.

Abilene died in her kitchen, reaching for a teacup. She hadn't been seen in two weeks; a neighbour finally noticed, made the landlord break in.

You hung up the phone, picked up your fork, put it down again. Put your hand to your eyes to block the sight of the crumbling shepherd's pie, the corn and carrots spewing messy from its centre, the congealing potatoes. Brent reached across the table and patted your hand, just another piece of the loss that had you doubled over in your chair, wailing like a mourner from a bad play.

When they finally found Abilene, they estimated she'd been dead for twelve days. You imagine she was wearing her pink marabou mules. Once they'd taken care of her — and by that, you understand they mean removed her, because by then there was no taking care of Abilene — the landlord had to replace the kitchen floor. Abilene was cremated immediately. At the church you stared at an empty altar.

You asked Abilene, once, why she and Leland didn't have children.

"We tried, but I couldn't." She shrugged. "I was sad for a while, but Lisa is like a daughter to me."

You spritzed her hair and took another small section, rolling your curling iron tight, laying your comb between it and her ear to protect her from the heat. "Now that we're getting married, I'm wondering if I want kids."

"I'm not sure, in retrospect, how sad I really was. I expected to have children. Then, when we couldn't, I expected to feel sad. So, I did." She smiled at you in the mirror. "I worked with Leland, helped him build the business. I don't feel I missed anything."

"You would have been a whole different lady," you said. "And I like you like this."

You wondered, though, how lonely Abilene was. Her life seemed small, errands parcelled out over the week. Church, hair appointments, paying bills at the bank — excuses to leave the house, to bring order to her days. You urged her to join a group, go to the seniors' centre. But she didn't want to spend time with old people. She said she didn't feel old.

This made you laugh at first, but it was the truth — she wasn't old. She looked old, and her cream polyester blouse with the floppy bow at the neck was definitely an old lady blouse, but the girl was just below the surface.

When Pastor Plage finished his meaningless non-eulogy, you scanned the faces in the church. A woman stood to the side in the entryway; elderly ladies murmured past, shaking her hand. Your voice shook as you approached her and spoke.

"Lisa?"

The woman smiled; her eyes were tired, red.

"Oh, Susan," she said. Her wool jacket was scratchy under your hands, her hair clean and floral, silky against your cheek. You breathed it in as you wept on her, and she wept on you. Then you moved to the church basement with Matthew, ate pâté and pickle sandwiches with the crusts cut off. You asked after Lisa's children, her husband, by name.

"Oh, Susan." There was a particular way Abilene said your name whenever she saw you or spoke to you on the phone. She said it flatly, with a downward inflection; it was a statement. She said it with the same particular note of satisfaction each time, as though she not only took pleasure in seeing you, but also in saying you.

Abilene missed two hair appointments. Jennifer didn't call to check either Saturday, and she didn't attend the funeral. And you wondered how much you had to do with her lack of concern, her lack of sorrow — never raising your price, forcing the stylists who came after you to work on Abilene for a proportionately lower fee, because which of them would have the nerve to double the cost of a shampoo and set for an elderly widow?

Six weeks after Abilene's death, you received a small package from Lisa. Within it was a sealed envelope addressed to you in Abilene's writing — her elegant old-school penmanship made shaky with age. Lisa found it while she was packing up Abilene's apartment, moving across that terrible new kitchen floor. She must have wanted to open it. She enclosed one of Abilene's anniversary rings — three tiny diamonds in an old-fashioned, heavy setting of dull gold. "Abilene would have wanted you to have it," Lisa wrote.

Abilene's letter was dated two days before her estimated death. She couldn't sleep. Nothing was wrong, she wrote, she just wasn't tired. She was up at three in the morning, thinking of you, of how nice it had been to see you at Christmas. She sent her love to Brent, to his mother, most of all to you. You slid the ring onto your pinky finger, put your head on the table, felt the placemat grow damp beneath your cheek.

You try now to think of Brent, of your former mother-in-law, in the context of Abilene. That's when they — and you, too — were their best, truest selves. Perhaps when Brent is an old man he will flirt gently with little old ladies. Perhaps, at those moments, he will remember it was Abilene who taught him the pleasures of courtliness.

You look at the hair of older women on the streets. Their sets are conservative, brushed out smoothly into silver waves. You have thought of asking your new lover to say your name the way Abilene did, of teaching him how, but you won't. Even if this new lover lasts, your name, said in that particular way, is gone.

After ten years, you are inching closer to forgiving Pastor Plage and Jennifer. They didn't know Abilene, even though one had her at his table, and the other wove her fingers through her hair. They didn't take the time. You did, eventually, but you're only too aware of how offhand and careless your own love has always been.

You dreamed Abilene's hair, many months after her death. You had moved into your new apartment and were sleeping alone again, relieved and terrified. You set Abilene's hair with care, spraying and curling, backcombing, smoothing it flat at the sides, sweeping the curls high on her head — a long, painstaking, detailed dream.

Abilene didn't speak; she just smiled at you in the mirror.

Exit interview #2

This weird little grey pod is set in the middle of the largest room in the art gallery — like that's a normal placement for a pod the size of one of those tiny campers that people pull behind their sedans — and it's here so people can step inside when they want to talk to dead people. Talk to dead people. Seriously.

There's a green wheelie chair, and a panel of buttons I can push that will allow a random dead woman to talk to me — to comfort me, to be specific.

This isn't by choice, believe me. I ducked in here to hide from Ashley's first-year painting instructor. Not that looking at someone's crappy art hanging in a public gallery could be categorized as stalking, but I didn't want to take the chance. I was supposed to be here with Ashley last week for opening night, celebrating her first showing as part of the college's annual student exhibition. Then two weeks ago she ghosted me. I have no idea why. So, when her instructor walked into the gallery this afternoon, I panicked. She's this tough-looking woman with long grey hair. She struck me as a militant feminist the only time I met her; I can see her going back to Ashley, saying she saw me creeping around her picture, looking sketchy. The instructor was walking straight toward me, the washroom was on the far wall of the adjoining gallery room, and I leapt for the nearest available doorway, which happened to be the entrance to a death pod.

And now I'm stuck in here, trying to guess how long the art instructor is going to hang around an empty gallery. I barely got a look at Ashley's painting before I had to bail — it was a self-portrait that looked nothing like the selfies she always posts. God, this pod is barely tall enough to stand in; the ceilings and walls are curved, no angles in the entire space — even the selection buttons are round.

I don't get art. I didn't get Ashley's paintings and I don't get how this weird interactive exhibit is art. According to the gallery lady, it's literally about talking to dead people — she called it an 'installation.' She also called herself a 'docent,' whatever the hell that is. She was bored and desperate for someone to walk in the door — as soon as I got here, she started telling me about it. I wasn't really listening, I just wanted to get in and out again before I saw anyone I knew. I skipped my last class to come early when it should've been safe. Not that my friends go to art galleries, but it wasn't inconceivable that I might run into some of my parents' friends, or some of our senior neighbours.

Two big monitors hang above the control panel. I jab randomly at a couple of buttons. I have no idea how long I should wait. This whole situation is lame — this stupid installation, me trapped here, cramped, all these bright, flashing buttons. Who would use this? This is what guy friends and beer were invented for.

That's what Connor and Jacob are for. After Ashley ditched me, they took me to our favourite sports bar and fed me whiskey shots and beer.

"That's fucking brutal, man," Jacob said. "Break-up by text. What a bitch."

"She changed her relationship status online five seconds after she texted me," I said. "She didn't even give me a chance to talk to her — to find out what was wrong."

Connor laughed. "Yeah, that's cold." He drained his glass and waved at the waitress for another round. "You're better off without her."

"It's humiliating," I said. "Why'd she have to rub it in so publicly, how happy she was to be rid of me? Who do you think saw it?"

Connor said, "Who cares what her friends think?" The waitress delivered three more shots and another jug of beer. They waited until she walked away then clinked their shot glasses against mine. "Fuck her. You're better off."

Jacob said, "I never liked that tramp-stamp bitch. Trying to get you to beg." He hoisted his shot glass in my direction, splashing whiskey on the already sticky table. "Please fucking tell us you didn't beg."

"I didn't," I said. "But I wanted to know what I'd done wrong."

Jacob said, "Dude. Dude, you begged. She turned you into a pussy." He lifted his shot glass to his mouth, and Connor and I followed suit. "Now it's time to man up."

I shot back the whiskey. It was cheap and skanky, and I choked when it hit the back of my throat. We got semi-drunk watching the ball game. When they pushed me out of the cab a couple hours later, Connor slapped my shoulder and said a few more nights out with the boys, and I'd be better than ever. If I'd had to take a shot every time he used the word 'better,' and every time Jacob told me to man up, I'd have ended up head-first in the toilet. The perfect new drinking game for guys.

Right now, Ashley's probably at the centre of some girl comfort huddle, probably remembering every casual word I ever spoke over the course of our relationship, pulling it all apart as proof of what an asshole I am. To be honest, I'm doing that, too — trying to figure out what I did that was so wrong, despite having nothing to go on other than my overactive imagination. Am I a terrible person? Have I done something unforgivable? I don't fucking know, and no one will tell me.

Copies of the artist statement sit in a holder that hangs from the console. I feel like an idiot, but I pull one out and start to read. It runs through the sort of truisms people post on Instagram: "Death robs us of the opportunity to say goodbye — to hear the words we crave or to say the words that are stuck in our throats."

But if I substitute 'ghosting,' yeah, that's pretty much accurate. Ashley robbed me of the opportunity to find out what I'd done wrong, if there was anything I could do to fix it. She texted me to say we were DONE, said she didn't want to talk. Before I'd finished reading the message, before my heart could even climb back down my throat, a notification popped up that she'd changed her online relationship status to 'single.'

I was all thumbs, texting her back — typos everywhere — saying I didn't understand, what had I done? I said I was sorry for whatever it was, I was willing to change, I just needed to know. Yeah, Jacob, I fucking begged.

Zero response. By the end of the night, she'd blocked me, like I was some kind of stalker.

As I look at the artist statement, I'm thinking, that's exactly right, I do have all these words stuck in my throat. I'm not sure what they are, but I can feel them lodged there, like some surprise chunk in what you thought was going to be a smooth sauce. For the past two weeks, my voice keeps getting oddly hoarse every time I say her name. It's embarrassing.

The statement says there are all sorts of different recordings and images people can choose from — and the control panel has buttons to adjust the lights in the pod, and places to plug in a phone or a memory stick so you can pull up your own photos on the screen. There are even stuffed animals scattered around the pod, fake pets that people can hold as they pretend to talk to dead people — a grey kitten, a brown dog with long, floppy ears, a couple of farm animals, and a big orange and red parrot.

I look at the multicoloured buttons. What the hell, right? I have to kill time until the art professor is gone. If anyone sees me, it's just a joke anyway, and no one is going to hear me — the gallery woman said the pod was soundproofed. She was also quick to tell me that alarms would go off if anyone tampered with the electronics, so maybe I look like a criminal, or a jerk. Maybe she saw what Ashley saw.

I turn on the first monitor, and up comes a gallery of photos of a woman — the dead woman who put this death pod together. She's probably close to my mother's age, but she's pretty hot — elegant and athletic all at the same time. I click on a close-up of this dead woman smiling into the camera. Her eyes are warm, she's looking at me like she loves me, but her eyes also seem sad, like my mom when she told me my grandfather died.

The second monitor lights up and shows a bunch of options — the whole range of what anyone might want to hear from a dead person, I guess. Messages to and from parents, husbands and wives, lovers, friends and children. There are a lot. These are the ones that catch my eye: *Absolution*; *What I Should Have Said*; *You Were Loved*; *Please be Happy*; *The Impact We Have Continues*; *People are Flawed*; *It's Not You, It's Me — Seriously*.

I curl my lip at the *It's Not You, It's Me* one and click randomly on *Please be Happy*. A box pops up telling me to select a voice — I can have the dead woman talk to me in almost any accent — Irish, Australian, you name it. There are some American options, too, including Boston American and Southern States. I leave it at the default, which I assume is the dead woman's actual voice.

"Mourning me doesn't mean you have to hold yourself in stasis," she says. Her voice is deep and soft and sexy, like an old movie star or one of those Anne Murray tapes my mom used to play when I was little. "My memory will always be with you, and you can bring me back any time you like through stories, photos, videos, songs — through all kinds of memories. But don't save yourself for me, as if I were coming back. You can honour me by continuing to say my name, and by being happy. Because seeing you happy always made me happy."

Yeah, right. This has zero to do with Ashley. But it makes that spot in my throat feel thicker anyway.

"Tell me what your concerns are," the dead woman says. Text flashes across the monitor, inviting me to speak into the microphone and press 'enter' when I'm done. I slap at the enter button, which is a light yellow colour.

"You know me so well," she says. "Think about what I would tell you right now if I were in the room with you." She asks what's making me push happiness away right now. She tells me to imagine myself and her — Ashley, I guess — sitting together in one of our favourite places, and to imagine the advice she would give me. I think this dead lady would be a lot kinder with her life advice than Ashley would be to me, but I can't imagine what either one of them would suggest I do. "I want you to be happy," she says.

The monitor asks me to reply again, and I hit the exit button.

I rub my hand over my face. This has nothing to do with me. I can't imagine Ashley talking to me in such a gentle, loving voice. I remember the huge feeling of satisfaction I had last year when I scored tickets to a Britney Spears concert for her birthday, knowing how excited she'd be. And she was ecstatic. It made me happy to give her that. But did it make Ashley happy to see me happy? Were we like that to each other most of the time?

I was there for her. I cheered her on when she wasn't sure about the art pieces she was working on. I don't know much about art, but I tried. I listened. I said it all looked good to me.

I hadn't actually seen the painting she put in the show until today. She talked about it a little when she was trying to decide which piece she was going to submit, but she wouldn't show it to me. To be honest, when I finally saw it, I was surprised — I wish I'd had more time to look from different angles. It's a self-portrait that doesn't look much like Ashley. I mean, I could tell it was her, but she looked like she'd just rolled out of bed after a rough night — no makeup, stringy hair. Ashley wouldn't be caught dead in public without makeup, so I don't get why she chose that piece to hang in public. If you saw that picture without knowing her, you'd never guess she's hot.

I punch another button: *Absolution*. Then, before I start the recording, I pull out my phone and plug it into the control panel.

I pull up a photo of Ashley on the monitor. I took it with my phone a few months ago — she's smile-laughing into the camera and tossing her hair, like she's mocking fashion models. That's not quite how the moment was, since I had to take about ten before she found one she'd let me keep. Seeing that bright smile makes my throat tighten again, and I stab at the button to start up the dead woman's voice.

"One of the benefits of someone dying is that memories of you behaving in ways you're not proud of can die with them," the woman says.

It's so unexpected, I laugh.

She goes on to say that's not an excuse to continue to behave badly, but that people need to let go of the past and focus on doing better in the future. She says the dead are owed nothing, but the living are owed a whole lot. She says that choosing to be better — to be kinder — with the living is the best way to let go of guilt about bad behaviour. Then she says again, "Think about what I would tell you right now if I were in the room with you." She says that what she saw is not the same as the story I'm telling myself, and I realize my hands are clenching into fists.

"But I don't have a clue what I did wrong," I say to Ashley. "I have no idea if I need forgiveness or not."

Her smile is frozen in place, that one slightly crooked tooth visible. She was always self-conscious about that flaw, no matter how many times I told her I thought it was cute. Well, that didn't need absolution, I think. The dead woman would definitely call that good boyfriend behaviour.

I pull the microphone toward me and turn it on.

"Please forgive me for reassuring you when you were insecure about your looks," I say. "Forgive me for sitting online for hours before Britney Spears tickets went on sale to make sure I got you the best seats I could afford. And please forgive me for putting your happiness ahead of my own."

It's strange, when you hear your voice over a mic — it reverberates, sounds deeper, richer, more important. I sound like a radio announcer, but a smarmy one, because the reverberation makes it clear that what just came out of my mouth is a stack of lies.

I lean toward the mic again.

"Come on," I say. "Who actually puts someone else's happiness ahead of their own? Maybe old people do, like parents or grandparents." God, Jacob called me pussy-whipped for going to Britney Spears with Ashley — can you imagine what he would've said if I'd acted like that all the time?

This is getting weird. I exit *Absolution*.

And then I work my way through *People are Flawed*. This time, I answer the dead woman's questions. I look at Ash's photo and think about how she was with me — the times she tried to talk about her feelings, and I teased her for being a tender little flower, and the times she wouldn't talk no matter how much I asked her. All the boring stories she told about her girlfriends. I think about how I was with her — how I rolled my eyes every time she glanced at me during the Britney concert, even though I actually like Britney, and how hard it was to stand still while Ashley danced, but I did anyway.

Also, how I said I thought her paintings were beautiful and I meant it.

Also, how I didn't deserve the way she broke up with me.

I lean into the microphone. "Honestly, I thought you were sort of high-maintenance, and a bit shallow." I pause, staring at the screen. "And I was glad when you switched to art," I say. "Because I didn't like that a person I thought was shallow got better grades than me in school."

She's smiling so widely her eyes are crinkled at the corners. She trusts me in this photo. Not like her expression the day she closed her bedroom door and stood in front of it, refusing to give me even a glimpse of her self-portrait.

My throat clogs with hoarseness again. I say, "I do miss you, Ash. And I did love you. Just not that much."

Somehow, I've ended up holding one of the stuffed animals while I'm doing all this talking and listening — my hand is gently brushing back and forth over the head of a brown and white goat, flipping its floppy ears back and forth.

If Jacob could see me right now, I'd never live this shit down. He'd tell me to man up, not to be a pussy.

My fingers sift through the silky tuft of hair between the goat's ears. I click around until the dead woman repeats the *People are Flawed* piece in a Scottish accent. I repeat and expand on the list of my flaws in the worst Scottish accent ever.

We all think we're good guys at heart, even when we're acting like dicks. Jacob would call himself a good guy, too. But good how? When we tell someone to be a man, what do we even mean?

The dead woman and I work through *The Impact We Have Continues* in fine southern drawls, and then I try it a second time in my own voice.

I look into Ash's happy crinkled eyes. My voice through the microphone sounds deep and resonant; it echoes around the pod, and the mic continues to emphasize the times when I'm being kind of a dick with my answers. My little goat buddy tips his horns at me approvingly whether I'm being honest or flippant.

The art professor must be gone by now. I clear the screen and unplug my phone from the control panel. Ashley's face disappears. I push back the green wheelie chair and look at the goat. On impulse, I stuff him in my pocket, then I walk out, back into the main gallery to find Ash's painting.

It's almost life-sized. Up close she's even more shattered than I thought at first glance. Ash's brushstrokes are broader and messier than usual, and she's added shadows in dull greens and greys in odd places on her face. I can't tell if she's angry or sad or exhausted.

Her artist statement doesn't make much sense to me, but I stuck it out with the dead lady's statement, so I tell myself I can get the hang of this new language, and I read it through slowly, twice. She talks about public versus private personas and the pressures on women to act and speak and look certain ways. It's all feminist stuff I've heard before. I feel like there's a secret message for me in here, but I don't understand how to decipher it.

If Jacob saw this painting, he'd make some asshole joke about why someone as hot as Ash would go out of her way to look unfuckable.

And when Ashley got mad, I'd laugh and tell her to relax, that's just how Jacob is. If I want to be honest — the way the woman in the grey pod asked me to be — that type of situation happened a lot. Jacob's version of manning up would take over the room, and I, Mr. Easygoing Good Guy, would tell everyone to chill, all the while avoiding eye contact with Ash so I wouldn't have to see her wounded expression.

The hoarse, scratchy feeling is clogging up the back of my throat again. I look down at my jacket pocket, see the fluffy edge of a brown and white hoof poking out. The docent woman walks through the arched entrance on the far side of the room, and I hold my breath until she exits through its opposite matching archway again.

If I can sneak the stolen goat back into the dead lady's pod before I leave the art gallery, maybe I'm not an irredeemable douchebag. And maybe this time I'll press the *What I Should Have Said* button, the one I avoided the first time I sat in the death pod. Or maybe I won't press the button; maybe this time I'll just say the words out loud: "Forgive me."

Acknowledgements

I have so many people to thank. Fran Kimmel and Joan Crate, for excellent and loving feedback. Paul Harris and Terry Warke for a Sunworks writing grant, and for always believing in this book. Barry Dempster for timely Tarot readings. Staff Sergeant Rob Marsollier of the Red Deer RCMP for answering my questions about what it's like to move through a city on fire. Any errors in the fire and smoke scenes in the title story are mine.

An early version of *The Brilliant Save* won the CBC Alberta Anthology Prize for Short Fiction and appeared on CBC Radio One and in *Alberta Anthology 2007*. *The Room of Pickled Foods* won the 2013 Sarah Selecky Little Bird competition and first appeared in Little Bird Stories Vol. III. Thanks to judge Alix Olin for selecting it. More thanks to Sarah Selecky for generous feedback on *An Old Lady and Her Hair* and *Exit Interview #1*. *Pickled Foods* was reissued in Little Bird Stories Vol. III in spring 2022 through Ascendant Press, an imprint of Invisible Publishing; thanks to editor Matteo Cerilli.

I worked on this book over many retreats at St. Peter's Monastery in Muenster, Saskatchewan. Love and thanks to: Fr. Demetrius Wasylyniuk, the sweetest monk in the world; Br. Pierre Rouillard, who bears no resemblance, other than the loan of his name, to the painter killed off in these pages; and Fr. Paul Paproski, whose gentle heart and terrible puns are deeply missed.

I'm deeply grateful to Aritha van Herk for intelligent, respectful editing and to Naomi K. Lewis for detailed copyedits. It was humbling to have women of such talent working with me this book. More thanks to the University of Calgary Press team: Brian Scrivener, Helen Hajnoczky, Alison Cobra, and to Melina Cusano for a brilliant cover design.

Thanks to the Canada Council and the Alberta Foundation for the Arts for grants that helped in the development of this book.

Most of all, thanks and love to Blaine Newton, first reader, fellow writer, life partner.

LESLIE GREENTREE is the author of the award-winning short story collection *A Minor Planet for You*. Her second book of poetry, *go-go dancing for Elvis*, was shortlisted for the Griffin Poetry Prize. Leslie co-wrote the play *Oral Fixations* with her life partner Blaine Newton, which was produced in 2014 by Ignition Theatre. She has won CBC literary competitions for poetry and fiction, and has been shortlisted for Writer's Guild of Alberta and Humber Creative Nonfiction awards.

BRAVE & BRILLIANT SERIES

SERIES EDITOR:
Aritha van Herk, Professor, English, University of Calgary
ISSN 2371-7238 (PRINT) ISSN 2371-7246 (ONLINE)

Brave & Brilliant encompasses fiction, poetry, and everything in between and beyond. Bold and lively, each with its own strong and unique voice, Brave & Brilliant books entertain and engage readers with fresh and energetic approaches to storytelling and verse.